THE
COUNTRY
BOY

THE COUNTRY BOY

The Story of His Own Early Life

HOMER DAVENPORT

with a new introduction by
WALT CURTIS

Powell's Press
PORTLAND, OREGON

in conjunction with

HOMER DAVENPORT–OREGON'S GREAT CARTOONIST
By Walt Curtis

Homer Davenport (1867–1912), the Silverton cartoonist, is one of Oregon's most extraordinary celebrities. Through the support of formidable newspaperman William Randolph Hearst, he would become the most influential political cartoonist in the U.S.A. Millions saw his cartoons. Hearst used his darling "Davvy" as a point man muckraking against political bosses and big trusts such as Standard Oil Company. Davenport cartoons, with direction from Hearst, ushered in the Progressive Era and promoted the ascendancy of the American Empire. Breaking with Hearst, Davenport helped reelect Teddy Roosevelt to the presidency in 1904. One might argue that he had more impact on the American way of life than radical journalist John Reed or poet-lawyer C.E.S. Wood, both Oregonians and players on the national scene.

Yet Homer Davenport's life is an enigma. Did this fantastic success bring him happiness? It is doubtful he ever would have left his beloved Silverton if his father Timothy W. hadn't cajoled, encouraged, and pushed his reluctant son toward a career in the arts. Homer remained homesick for his small town on the edge of the Willamette Valley all of his life.

The Country Boy, published in 1910, is an Oregon classic of small-town American life. The book is the coming-of-age memoir of a mid-1880s Oregonian, which parallels the coming of age of millions of Americans on the brink of the Twentieth Century. *The Cleveland Leader* said, "Davenport's *The Country Boy* belongs on the shelf with Mark Twain's books." Privately printed, it might have become a bestseller if it had been properly distributed. After all, Homer Davenport was a household name. Like Norman Rockwell paintings and Garrison Keillor's "Lake Woebegon," *The Country Boy* was already nostalgia when it appeared. Except in Davenport's world, these aren't middle-class pretensions. As a work of literature, this true-life memoir is droll, surprising, sentimental, and vaudevillian. Often, the author is the butt of his own description.

Homer's life from the very beginning is improbable. When his mother Florinda Geer was pregnant, she obsessed on Thomas Nast cartoons in *Harper's Weekly*. She was convinced that one day her son would become as famous as Nast. To this end, she followed the recommended proper diet and deep concentration in the medical essay "How To Born A Genius" by Dr. Russell Trall. Young Homer, born March 8, 1867, was sketching pigs and horses on the Geer homestead in the Waldo Hills by age three and a half. This property is today a "century farm," and the renowned "Riding Whip Tree," which the boy played under, still stands. It grew from a cottonwood switch pushed into the ground by his mother,

Tragedy suddenly struck the pioneer Davenport family in 1870. An outbreak of smallpox attacked the community. Florinda was fatally stricken. The pox left Homer's face scarred, but the death of his beautiful mother was life-altering. Florinda was 33 years old. The antique-looking photograph of mother and son is the frontispiece to *The Country Boy*. Florinda's dying words to her husband went: "You must take another wife, but . . . my prophecy . . . my dream . . . my little son will be a cartoonist. Give him every opportunity."

Dad's perseverance and patience is the stuff of sainthood. The story of the cartoonist is also the father's. They bonded, perhaps because of the mother's death. Why did the Davenports move to Silverton, a town of 300 inhabitants? Homer was 7 years old. The father had given up a beautiful 1851 farm he loved, carved from the Oregon wilds, so his son could have a future "in the Latin Quarter of that village."

Timothy was a well-educated professional who held numerous high-profile jobs—Indian agent, Oregon State Representative, and land agent. He played the violin and loved the classics. His son must've pained him sorely those first 25 years, the period of time covered by *The Country Boy*. All he required from Homer, besides milking the cows, was to "study faces and draw." The townsfolk cannot understand why this strapping, healthy young man is lounging around, doing nothing.

As with everything Homer Calvin Davenport did, the apocryphal and the anecdotal can't do justice to real events. Truth outstrips storytelling. For 70 years, rare book dealers searched for the title *The Belle of Silverton, and Other Oregon Stories* (1888–1889), tale of a girl he incapably courted. The book didn't exist. As a joke, the author included it in the short bibliography of his works. I am indebted to *Homer Davenport of Silverton* (1973), the accurate biography compiled by

Oregon's great bookman Alfred Powers and researcher Leland Huot. It is a detailed account of his life and career in a limited edition of 700.

Powers and Huot sort out the many false starts, numerous part-time jobs young Homer held before going to San Francisco. He was a jockey in Salem and became a clown in McMahon's one-ring circus. Maybe he learned to draw the Republican elephant and the Tammany tiger there. He slept on pool tables and posted handbills on walls for Clara Morris in *Camille*. Sister Adda and he cried all the way through the tearjerker. Dad sent him to Armstrong Business School in Portland, and he failed.

Before cartooning, railroading was his most consistent job. He was a wiper on the shiny No.8 engine, as his bull terrier Duff rode upfront on the cowcatcher. Trains gave the country boy freedom and access to the world. At the freight office in West Stayton Homer sketched a portrait of his best friend "Duffy" on the wall. Years later, firefighters saved the drawing, shouting, "Let the damned building go, but save the cartoon!"

About 1890 Homer started his career in Portland. He sketched the steamboat "Harvest Queen," running the Cascade rapids on the Columbia for *The Oregonian*. No pay. He struggled with spelling, and many of his cartoon captions needed correction.

The big break came in January of 1891. *The Portland Sunday Mercury,* a sporting weekly, put him on a train for New Orleans to cover the Dempsey-Fitzsimmons fight. Jack (Nonpareil) Dempsey was a popular middleweight champion from Portland. Homer brought back an alligator that froze in Denver and game-cocks that made it to Silverton—"Dempsey" and "Fitzsimmons." His 21 views of the fight were said to have been extremely accurate. They are now "lost," but on the trip his skills—verbal, social, and artistic—emerged. Destiny intervened.

NO HONEST MAN NEED FEAR CARTOONS.

In 1892, his father sends him to San Francisco, prepared to attend art school. The rural youth is in shock, alone in an alien world. A relative, C.W. Smith, a general manager at the Associated Press, got the Davenport boy a letter of introduction to the *San Francisco Examiner*—the Hearst paper. Davenport actually went to work, earning two dollars and fifty cents a week at *The Examiner*. Formally trained staff artists ridiculed his home-spun style. He later worked briefly at The Chronicle. He's 25 years old.

Finding it hard to settle down, he yearns to go to the Chicago World's Fair—the Columbian Exposition. Again Smith of Associated Press helped him land a job with the *Chicago Daily Herald*. Romantic interest Daisy Moor visited, and they're soon married. The Panic of 1893 took him back to San Francisco and *The Chronicle* art department. A rivalry between the two papers was going on, and Homer's popular work caught Hearst's attention, who soon offered him $75 a week, a princely sum at the time.

Davenport's small town ethics, largely absorbed from his father, inspired his cartoons. The skill that Davenport possessed was a photographic eye and a naturalistic style. He could look at someone, draw a realistic cartoon, and divulge the person's character. Hearst published his portrait of Sam Rainey, the powerful political boss never previously portrayed, filling the entire front page of *The Examiner*. Influential politicos in California both feared and admired the caricatures. They wanted to hang them on the wall, as well as beat him up!

The relationship between Hearst and Davenport evolved into something remarkable. They were like brothers! Hearst was his boss, but also his strongest advocate. The Powers-Huot biography reports:

"A paper in the East wants me to join it," he told Hearst.

"What does the paper offer?"

"A hundred a week."

"My God, Davvy, that's as much as the managing editor gets."

"I sure hate to leave you, Mr. Hearst."

"Davvy, you're not leaving," Hearst replied.

In October of 1895, the hotshot publisher called his brilliant editor Arthur Brisbane and cartoonist Davenport to New York City. This team of young men would change the business! Shake up the world. *The Evening Journal* increased its circulation to a million in 6 years. In this time of mogul capitalism and American jingoism, Hearst's paper flamboyantly exposed the trusts and the graft of political bosses. Of course, this was done to sell newspapers. Populism in full swing, the American people were hungry for social and political justice.

Davenport was in demand and made tons of money. His work was syndicated on both coasts. At the height of his career, he was making $25,000 a year, the same salary as the President. Davenport's Uncle Sams were the most expressive and reassuring ever done. The American people could relate to this tall, Lincolnesque leader lecturing Boss Hanna's "The Brute," holding the hand of the waif Cuba during the Spanish-American War. Homer restored Admiral Dewey's popularity after his marriage to a rich widow. His cartoons reflected the troubled, empire-building era. Hearst was a genius at yellow journalism and his mother's silver dynasty millions paid the bills in his press war with Joseph Pulitzer.

A bit of an egomaniac, Citizen Hearst tried for the Democratic nomination to the presidency, and failed. After personally meeting candidate Theodore Roosevelt—noting his energy and charisma—Davenport abruptly left Hearst's paper, *The New York Journal,* in mid-1903. He would not go back until 1911, a year before his death. The Republicans paid him $1,000 a week for six months. They spent $200,000 circulating the largest vote-getting cartoon in the history of American politics. Davenport drew Uncle Sam with his hand on the shoulder of T.R., and the caption "He's Good Enough For Me."

After Homer left Hearst, Major Pond—Twain's booking agent—sent him out on the lecture circuit. He ensconced

"HE'S GOOD ENOUGH FOR ME"

the family first at East Orange, New Jersey, and later on the "Davenport Estate," a stud farm at Morris Plains.

In his biography *HOMER, The Country Boy* (1986), horse lover Mickey Hickman, a Silverton resident, documents every aspect of Davenport's fascinating book *My Quest of the Arab Horse* (1909). Both books are treasure troves of Arabian horse lore. President Roosevelt's personal letter to the Sultan of Turkey asked for an "Irwade," a special permit authorizing his friend Homer to import the Arabians. It made sense that the White House "Rough Rider" would be interested in such an adventure.

Hickman rediscovered the glass slides and lantern projector Davenport used in his lectures when he returned from the desert. The photographs of Homer on a camel, his friend Akmet Haffez, the encampment of wild Anazeh Bedouin preparing for war—this is the stuff of Lawrence of Arabia. As a present of brotherhood, he is given Wadduda, the favorite war mare of Sheik Hashem Bey, along with her keeper Said Abdallah. By Allah, the coincidences continue! Till then, no brood mare was allowed outside of the Ottoman Empire. The 27 pureblooded

Arabians he imported enhance the bloodlines of America's most famous horses.

The 1906 journey by Davenport to the Anazeh Bedouins was the highpoint of his life. He secretly drew the Sultan, a feeble old man, and hid the drawing in a bale of hay. The temperature was 135 degrees in the shade of the tent. Overcome by emotion, Homer realizes: "Ever since a small boy, I knew that I was just as much of an Arab as any in the desert. I had been one of its members all of my life."

Akmet Haffez seals the deal – Davenport has another Arabian.

Among these restless people, Davenport experienced something transcendental, beyond time.

Back in Morris Plains, the Bedouin stable boy Said Abdallah slept with the horses. There were pens and aviaries of exotic birds. Davenport commuted to work everyday on the Millionaire Special . . . the lifestyle of the Rich and Famous. The 27 acres of hill, wood, and stream possessed a huge stable and stalls for his prized Arabians. The modest farmhouse had a back porch with 2 clapboard walls, autographed by boxers, actors, and artists at his annual barbecue. Buffalo Bill and his troupe came out on the commuter train, as did Lillian Russell, boxers Fitzsimmons and John L. Sullivan, and the lavishly gowned Flora-Dora girls.

Great men trusted him instinctively. Even enemies like Boss "Dollar Sign" Hanna forgave his insults. Davenport's eyes were tired and all-knowing. He comfortably wore an old slouch hat. No longer a country boy, but a sophisticated man. Davenport genuinely liked people and, chameleon-like, had the ability to get along with everyone, except his spouse. The beautiful and fashionable Daisy did not like Silverton, especially when he took her there to honeymoon.

Davenport was also a spiritualist. His father believed in an afterlife. There are strong elements of predestination in his life, work, and tragic death. The fatal flaw was the marriage. Homer Jr. sided with Daisy. Davenport wanted a peaceful separation from her, because she was a good mother. He wrote his father in July of 1907: "I am sickened and tired of the meaningless conversations. I have taken a great change, growth toward a higher plain, in which there is happiness." By March 1909, he was out of the house at Morris Plains, on the edge of a nervous breakdown. Famous ex-professional baseball pitcher A.G. Spalding offered an oasis in San Diego.

He deeded everything to his wife. Still she was suing for alimony. Under doctor's care, he thought of lecturing again. Catherine Tingley, the leading authority on theosophy, at the Raga Yoga Colony was a spiritual mentor. He relieved himself of his sorrows in the *San Diego Sun* of Feb. 3, 1910, in a rambling 3-page article—"Davenport Explains Troubles With Wife." Somehow he pulled himself together to publish *The Country Boy*. He had fallen in love with a mysterious woman named Zadah. When Hearst heard that Davenport wanted to work again, he wired him a one-liner: "Dear Davvy: Come home. Hearst."

Everything was looking up, in spite of his father's death in 1911. Davenport felt positive about the upcoming divorce trial. He would be free to marry. Instead, Hearst sent him to cover the survivors from the sinking of the Titanic. He drew a great hand rising out of the water and pulling the ship under.

He suffered a nervous collapse, and was convalescing at the home of Mrs. Cochran . . . well known in mediumistic circles as ASSONATH NEYPA. At the end, the eight doctors in attendance couldn't save him from pneumonia. He died on May 2, 1912 at 45. Was fatalism at work? Every element in his life was coming together. Yet suddenly Davenport is dead, one year after his father's demise almost to the day.

Hearst paid for the funeral expenses. Davenport's great gray rectangular tombstone, paid for by popular subscription, was inscribed: "Erected by his friends to the Memory of Oregon's world-renowned Cartoonist." Pictured on the back was "The Journey Across"—showing a man in a chariot driven by an angel. Looking back on his earthly home, Silverton. Homer sketched the image when his father died and commented: "The saddest trip West I ever made . . . as I drew it in en route. It also depicts an important change in his life for the better." He was buried next to his beloved father.

*Homer's beloved father Timothy
in an 1894 portrait*

Fate works its maneuvers in strange ways. A mother's prophecy came true! Homer was blessed as an artist with the incomparable gift of seeing and drawing. A country boy's dream of owning and riding desert stallions was life-defining. Ninety years after his passing, Silverton still honors the prodigal son every August with oompah bands performing in the park and amateur art shows—Homer

Davenport Days. The humble yet thoroughly humorous account you are about to enjoy was written by a 43-year-old author at the height of a fabulous career to recapture the memories evoked by his beloved hometown throughout an amazing life.

Walt Curtis is Portland's unofficial poet laureate. He is the author of numerous small-press books, including The Erotic Flying Machine, The Roses of Portland, Rhymes For Alice Blue Light, *and* Mala Noche. *The last book was the source for Gus Van Sant's first feature film, and in 1995 he starred in Bill Plympton's documentary* Walt Curtis: The Peckerneck Poet. *For 30 years, he has co-hosted a poetry program, "The Talking Earth," on KBOO-FM radio in Portland. Curtis is the current secretary and one of the founders of the Oregon Cultural Heritage Commission.*

THE
COUNTRY
BOY

DEDICATED
TO THE SACRED
MEMORY OF MY
MOTHER
AND
TO MY DAUGHTER
GLORIA

PREFACE

THIS book deals with just an ordinary boy, brought up, however, among people and conditions that were not ordinary. This little town of Silverton and the neighborhood around it were made up of men and women who had left the best sections of the Eastern States to go West that they might avoid the Railroads and conditions that followed them. Strange as it may seem one of the early settlers of Silverton had moved from Connecticut to Illinois to get away from the railroad, and later from Illinois to Oregon, and finally died in Silverton without ever having seen a railroad train. Such a statement might mislead some people into thinking that the man was a crank, but that was not the case. On the contrary he was a man of distinctive type, of much nobility of purpose, that had just happened in his early youth to imagine that he would not like railroading. And the people that followed his example were people of good blood and in some instances of high education and all in all they made up a fine average community. More than likely many small towns in New England two hundred years ago were like Silverton was twenty years ago, but a town like Silverton was then would be hard to locate nowadays, and the Silverton of to-day is in few respects like the fine old dignified town of even 1885. They were the pioneers and the first generation. To-day it's different. The old Silverton was given a certain dignity by a very large and remarkably shaped old oak tree that stood in the center of the Main Street; how old it was no one knew but it had been the shade for the Molalla and

Santiam Indians for unknown generations and was more than likely in the direct route of these Indians who went to and fro from the Council of the Great Multuomah Tribe on the Columbia River prior to the falling of "the bridge of the Gods." The old oak, as everybody called it, was a stately giant, and the early settlers of Silverton looked a fitting people to group themselves under it and around it, and, as I have said, it was the superb character of both men and women that made Silverton, the old town, so distinctly different.

The tree and town were nearly all destroyed once by fire. A merchant named Alex Ross let a lighted candle brush against his beard and from his whiskers the blaze leaped madly into the lace curtains of his store window and one of the handsomest city blocks was soon burnt to the ground. The town then got a hook and ladder company, and a fire brigade was organized with a tower and a fire bell on top of it. Years passed and passed and the firemen grew older and less attentive at the annual fire drill. The fire department consisted of a hose, hook and ladder wagon with some fine axes with gilding on the blades, some long leather buckets, a long hose, and some fire helmets. Some ten years after the first fire another broke out, in the old brick store; possibly from a cigar stub as a man was seen smoking one that day in the store. At any rate the old store was first to burn. The department was hard to arouse as the fire started at 2 a. m. or thereabouts. Dr. Davis was awakened by the glare of light. He thought he had overslept and that it was sun-up. Fully awake he ran to ring the fire bell, but little by little the farmers had cut off the rope to tie their teams till it was out of the doctor's reach. He threw rocks at the bell but was nervous and excited and only hit it once, so resorted to yelling "Fire!" on the principal streets until his voice gave out. Silverton was noted as a place to get sleep and rest in and the doctor was winded and hoarse before he awoke many of the old settlers. They found the hose gone, some one had borrowed it to irrigate his garden; the leather buckets were all gone. We had had one in our parlor for years with moss and "everlasting flowers" in it as an ornament, and the only things they found to fight the flames with were three of the company's fire helmets, and these came in handy to keep off the heat, as a whole row of wooden buildings were on fire, to say nothing of 50,000 cedar shingles, and it was nearly noon before the fire burned itself out when it came to the sparse settlement. But the backbone of the town was there yet and the pioneers were not all gone. They would go on determined not to be stopped by a fire. In fact bluffs seldom got away with much there, and I can cite one instance that was truly Silverton in every sense. A "Campbellite" minister by the name of Clark Braden came there to conduct a revival meeting. He was a man of quite some force and reputation, and a big quiet audience greeted him at his first hearing. He got on all right until near the close when he issued a sweeping challenge to any infidels or free thinkers to debate with him in Silverton. His utterances had hardly cleared his beard when ten men at least were on their feet asking him if he would debate with Robert G. Ingersoll. The preacher said "yes with him or any of his disciples." The meeting broke up with much excitement and promise, and within a few hours quite a long telegram, the longest ever sent out of Silverton was on its way East to Col. Ingersoll, and before long a brief one returned saying that Mr. B. F. Underwood was on a train for Silverton as a representative of Col. Ingersoll to debate for ten days with Rev. Clark Braden. They were to speak every evening, each man having one hour's time. That was typical of the early founders of Silverton. No admission was charged, and the occasion was carried on with much dignity until the last evening's debate when somebody started something, and when it was over several of the best families in town were on terms unbecoming to neighbors; but even this only lasted a few months and all the differences of a stormy night had passed. The manhood and womanhood that had brought them together during the hardships and trials of a pioneer life, in the covered-wagon days, had brought about a brotherhood that was after all too strong a bond to be broken by even religious whims and differences, and they were soon back together as one big family. All men and women who in their higher spiritual selves were even more religious in the truer form than the minister that had started the trouble, they were genuinely under the atmosphere and living in it that the old blind Arab poet described in his verse written during the eleventh century and saying, "when young, my friends I would defame, if our religious faiths were not the same, but now my soul has traveled high and low, now all save love to me is but a name." I only cite this incident as it was so typical of the place and went to show that the older pioneers of Silverton could start on short notice without even a rehearsal. But, oh, how I loved, and still love Silverton.

I could never expect to find another such community. Where else could one find a firm like Coolidge and McClaine, starting in partnership without a bookkeeper. They never even kept a pencil account of things. When Jake McClaine saw his partner with a new pair of pants on, whether he, McClaine, needed any or not, he took from the store a pair just to balance the books, and that was their method. They played fair with each other, starting with some calves they bought in the fall of the year, and from that deal this firm grew and grew until now, incorporated into a stock company, it is one of the biggest on the Pacific Coast; and when "call money" rents for big premiums in New York City, money that started in Silverton with these pioneer bankers comes in large quantities to Wall Street to reap the benefit of the quick loan system. But the Silvertonites of old, Coolidges, McClaines, Davis's, Browns, DeGuires, McGuires, Smiths, Tuggles, Blackerbys, Hibbards, Riches, Wolfards, Skaifes, Drakes, Ramsbys, Huttons, Thurmans and Simerals are getting thinned out, and in their places new faces from the middle west and south are coming. The first generation were not the stuff of their parents; conditions had changed, some of the younger men were bigger business men than their fathers yet they lacked a lot of a certain kind of character that made the fathers more interesting than any of their sons. The railroad and interurban trolleys change the conditions of things greatly, and Silverton has been no exception to this rule. The departure and arrival of the old Salem stage used to be an event, more than the trains coming and going to-day, but to me Silverton will always remain the same with no other memory second. I remember well my first impression of Silverton. I had come to town with my father and grandmother Davenport. It must have been when I was between four and five years old. We were stopping at the Coolidges', father had gone on beyond Silverton to survey for Scott Hobart, and in the evening of a great day, as grandmother and "Aunt Frank" Coolidge sat rocking and visiting on the back porch, I got their permission to go on to the sidewalk some distance from their big house. I remember I was all dressed up with new little boots that had copper toes. I followed the sidewalk to the old covered bridge and finally ventured through it, and there saw a great city for once without grandmother holding me. I was in a trance of delight watching it, when a big handsome man, named Marshall Dudley, came up to me and in a bass voice, said: "Are you so and so." I said, "yes." "What then are you doing in Silverton alone? You get back to Aunt Frank Coolidge's as hard as you can run." I did and found to my horror that I had bumped a copper toe off one of my new boots somewhere enroute.

From that moment Silverton has always been to me the greatest city in the world. I saw in it that evening a dignity, possibly radiating from the giant oak tree, that no other place ever could have. Its people were so kind, its stores filled with such good things, and the scenery back of it so beautiful. And the roar of the water falling over the Mill Dam gave it a thrill never to be forgotten by me. For years it held me in that trance. It inspired me to draw pictures, and day after day, month after month I used to draw its people on the smooth surface of the pine boxes that brought dry goods to the town, and, strangely, many of them I mounted on fiery Arabian steeds, and the strangest part of Silverton is that it never releases me a day from its hold. A day never passes that I don't hurry over its streets and see its last remaining pioneers, and in my vision replace those that have gone. I yet hear the roar of Silver Creek as it pours like a sheet of silver over the Mill Dam below the "old red shop"; then again I see it each day as the years go by as I first remember seeing it the evening I lost the copper toe from the new boot. I have thought of it while seated in the ruins of the Coloseum at Rome, thought of it in London and Paris and Constantinople, thought of it while resting in the death-like silence of the shadow of the Sphinx, and told of it near the Euphrates River in Arabia, while among the wild tribes of Anezeh. Even left its paper, "The Silverton Appeal," among that tribe.

I have told people of this little town's beauties till they have yawned and finally left in disgust, yet it holds me with a something that I cannot describe. Strangely I find that I have forgotten all the many rainy days, the boyhood fights and the neighbor quarrels. They with the petty pains and pangs of life have been forgotten, and while I know that some of my expressions of love for this little town have been misunderstood by the newer and younger generation, yet I am certain that the pioneers, the men and women that belong to the old oak tree, have all seen in every word I have ever written or line I have ever drawn pertaining to Silverton and the farmers around it, nothing but love. All the attention I have drawn to it in the past and any I may in the future was, will be, to benefit Silverton. My only regret is that we couldn't have remained always the same as we were before the big oak tree was chopped down, as that tree seemed to fit into our landscape better than open or paved streets do. The tree seemed to be a center of dignity around which we could build, a tree with stories beyond the first white man it ever saw; and many a day when I have watched the leading citizens playing marbles in its extensive shadow, I have thought: How many are the interesting stories *you* could tell, of ages passed when you saw the beautiful deer and other wild game gather at your base, of the great pride you must have felt when the old cock grouse hooted from your moss covered limbs in the early breaking of spring and of the interesting councils of war which painted Indians in ancient days convened under your spreading old limbs. Who knows but what the great Snohomish, the chief and orator of the Santiams, made your shade a stopping place going up the Columbia to the great council? At last you saw the first white man and his ox team approach, and later make treaty and trade and war with the Indians; and at the very last, you find you have been chosen as the center around which men and women of the finest type build a beautiful little city that for a time nestled under your very branches for protection. You grew and spread and at last as a mother that had walked the floor nights with her babe, cared for it in storms, furnished a cool shade for it in summer, were now in the way. Your limbs had tried to climb into the upper window of one of your children's stores. That was enough, a new element had come to town on a railroad, to make Silverton like other towns, so the giant tree heard its fate from a jury that were strangers. The tree might have called for help, but its real friends, the old pioneers, were away. Some of them each passing year had been driven by it, across the old covered bridge never to return, and others were out of town on their adjoining farms. The giant oak, the tree that had the beautiful stories to tell, was voted "guilty" and was slain. That evening as its huge branches were divided among the town's people, a small party of big men gathered at the stump of the tree. They were mad men and sad men as they realized that Silverton had to change, that a newer element with higher collars and smaller hats was in command. Many of their best and bravest citizens had already gone beyond the call of human voice, others would soon follow, and the tree, being one of them, had, also, made obeisance to the demand of society, fashion and wealth. From that day the dignity of Silverton began to wane. Thus I shall not wonder after I write of and draw the beauties of dear old Silverton, as I have done in this book, if by some I am misunderstood; but I shall never desert Silverton; it is my home and always will be. To me the old oak tree always stands and under it the men play marbles. The pioneers and their families that made it so full of character are still in their prime of life, the first beautiful girl I ever saw is still there just as beautiful as ever, and in the streets I yet hear the latest marches by the old Silverton band, the stores are still aglow with rich beauties. That's why I love it so dearly and that's why it's yet home to me.

HOMER DAVENPORT.

New York, June 17, 1910.

THE DIARY
OF A COUNTRY BOY

CHAPTER I

IT was getting late one evening on the farm in the Waldo Hills, Oregon; we were all sitting around the fireplace; it was fall, and while not cold, it was very damp. Father had been to town that day and he was discussing with my stepmother and my grandmother the advisability of going to Silverton to live. He said that every time he went to town lately Tom Welsh wanted him to move down and take charge of the Grange store.

It was a great evening, if it was rainy. I got out of Grandmother's lap and turned to the hired man and said, "Just think of it, we are going to Silverton maybe, to live right in the heart of the town." Finally I had to go to bed, though I wasn't a bit sleepy and I don't remember of sleeping a wink that night, but at the first excuse of daylight, I was up and off to the neighbors and relatives to tell them the news. It had stopped raining, and was as clear and beautiful as could be. I stood up on a rail fence and looked all over the country for miles around as far as the eye could reach, over the landscape I knew so well; in fact, the only one I knew. I could hear the bell on the engine at Salem twelve miles away, so clear was the atmosphere. Although early in the morning, my chapped feet didn't hurt me as usual, so from one uncle's house I went to another and around until I had told all my cousins that we were going to Silverton to live, that I was sorry, I hated to leave them, but the demand was great. The city was calling for us and we would perhaps have to go.

At Grandmother Geer's I found Grandmother Davenport, who had beat me over. She was old, but as spry as a sixteen-year-old girl. As the two grandmothers stood side by side on the porch as I approached, I thought of what two perfect women they were. The earth's surface could

have been combed and two finer types of womanhood could not have been found. As I had no mother, these two old ladies had reared me, and in a way they seemed more like mothers than grandmothers.

Up to this time the feeling of delight had made it possible for my bare feet just to touch the high places, but here at Grandmother Geer's things took on a serious aspect. I yelled to them, "Halloa," as I was opening the old gate that led past the big yellow rose bush, and all they did was to let their heads lop over on the one shoulder and smile. When I came closer and drew a long breath, Grandmother Geer said, "Homer, you and Grandma aren't going to leave me, are you?" All I did was to nod and ask her if she had any cookies, when Grandmother Davenport broke down and commenced to sob. Finally we all sat down, I with the cookies and the rest with long faces. Granny Geer said, "Well,

Grandpa will get rid of all the chickens if you're going, we won't have any one to hunt eggs, and no one to go with me to dig dandelion greens; and we won't see any boy riding the old red bull to the State Fair again, will we, Grandma?" Then they both broke down and cried. "But I'll come up and gather the eggs for you, it's only five miles," and I told her maybe we wouldn't go until spring anyway, and things had become so sad by this time that I thought I had better go on to the next neighbor's; so I left them with their heads on each other's shoulders, saying something in low tones.

In a few days father returned again from Silverton and said he had promised that he would take the Grange store in the spring. It seemed as though winter would never pass; it actually lasted years. We talked of nothing else during the evenings, and I thought of nothing else, dreamed of nothing else during the nights. Finally as spring opened we thought of Old John, a big, fat; round bay horse with knowing brown eyes. In fact, he was one of the family; all of us except my own mother and father had learned to ride and drive with Old John, as had all the neighbors' children. It wouldn't do to take him to Silverton, as he was afraid of covered bridges and bass drums, and they had one of each in that place.

Father didn't want to leave the farm he had chosen, of all the wilds of Oregon, in 1851. But my stepmother knew it was the only thing to do especially for my art education, which had already begun. I heard Father and Mother in arguments, and heard Father say that the city was no place to teach art; that art was most in evidence in the country, especially such a country, but women always win, so later in the spring my father sold the most beautiful farm I ever saw that we could move to Silverton, a town of three hundred inhabitants; that I might live in the Latin Quarter of that village, and inhale any artistic atmosphere that was going to waste.

Old John was left at Grandma Geer's with their Old Charley, a horse nearly as old but not half as smart. When the folks moved to Silverton they left me in the hills, after all, till my school was over, and I stayed with Grandmother and Old John, who didn't understand it.

I rode him to Silverton a Sunday or two, but we both felt strange. In the pasture we were at home, but the noise of Silverton and strange horses and boys and girls didn't make us feel just right. I knew Alvin McClaine, and one or two others, and everybody knew Old John, and most of them were glad we were coming. Alvin told me what we would do when I came to town, but Old John had to be left.

He had grown up in our family, Father got him when he was an orphan colt, and my own mother made a pet out of him. He was smart. He used to get into the milk-house and drink up all the milk. When he had done that, you could always find him in canyon pasture. It was the farthest away from the house. He could open any gate that farmers made, and they made the best; he could even open the doors to the house.

Up to the time of my mother's death, in 1870, he belonged exclusively to her, and she had taught him to return from Salem alone, a distance of twelve miles, with the buggy, and never was the vehicle injured. They used to take his bridle off and tie a card, explaining, on the back band of his harness, so that if he met strangers they wouldn't stop him, and those who knew him only spoke to him and smiled as he passed. Sometimes if he struck a good patch of clover in the fence corner, he would be a little late whinny-ing at the gate; but he never failed. Once on his return he made the philosopher of the place think, as he came home with pond lilies in the floor of the buggy. There were no ponds or streams in the Waldo Hills containing pond lilies, nor were there any in Salem, and it required deep thought.

He had gotten home so late that the only evidence they had were the lilies and scum from some pond, but the next morning they found he had been in mud up to his barrel; then they solved the problem. They had sent him away from Salem without water; the horse, knowing of Lake Labish on the lower road, eight miles out of his way, went there; its banks are steep and the bottom is very muddy, so the weight of the buggy on the slippery banks pushed him in when he went to drink. So he swam in a half circle to get back out, the floor of the buggy picking up the pond lilies on the swim.

He was a smart old fellow; in fact, he and Father were the thinkers of the place; it was on him I learned a lot, and between him and the ground I learned a lot more. I remember one awfully dark night I grew more than attached to him; it was my duty to get up the sheep, and that particular day I had been

playing so hard I forgot them. I was asleep, when they woke me to find out if I was sleeping, and then they asked if I had washed my feet; I was certain I had, but on bringing a candle it proved that I was mistaken as to the date. While I was sitting with just the ends of my toes in a basin of cold well water, trying to get up courage enough to shove in the whole foot, Father happened to think of the sheep and he

called out, "Are the sheep up?" I had forgotten them. It was dark and I heard an owl screech up in the orchard. Shedding tears didn't save me, I was ordered to the barn to get Old John. I had both hands clenched tight in his mane. I knew he was tracking the sheep. Presently from out the dark ahead I could hear the bell; then I knew that they would start straight for the barn, which they did. Once back in the stall I hugged Old John, the tears on my cheeks had dried with fright, and after a footbath I was in bed, safe from an awful, dark night, a coyote, and some barn and timber owls.

But Old John and I had some pleasant times; our associations were not all ghastly. In the summer we used to buck straw from the threshing machine; when there were picnics I used to braid his mane and tail the day before. Then when I rode to the picnic with his kinky mane, both of us used to

enjoy it, and he especially seemed to know how pretty he looked. But some way he was always so glad to get home; he didn't seem like another horse, he just seemed like one of the family, and the only time it took a man to handle him was when we went to the State Fair at Salem. When we got within half a mile of the fair grounds, where he could hear the boom of the bass drum in the distance, he turned into a wild horse; his ears were ever in motion then and his hazel eyes had the sparkle of an Arab's. He would try to cramp the buggy and get home, and at the State Fair it was always best to lead him, as he pranced all the time. But he was not mean; he didn't like state fairs, that was all. He and I stayed at Grandma's until just before I left to go to Silverton. Old John had been turned out on what we called "The Snake Hill Pasture," and there he and Old Charley were spending their last days. He was past twenty, as sound as a dollar, his only fault being that he was a little too fat and lazy. Grandfather had been over to the pasture to put out some squirrel poison; it was on Sunday, the last Sunday. I was to go to Silverton that afternoon. At the dinner table Grandfather spoke of the queer actions of Old John; said

that he acted strange, that he first noticed him whinnying long and loud; then he would stop and listen, first with one ear forward, then with the other. His eye had a sparkle that it never had, except at a state fair, and he seemed nervous. "He came to me and nosed at all my pockets, to see if I had salt for him; then he would try to play; colthood seemed to return to him, but in the midst of his play he would stop and call; he would even try to look at the sun, and when I came to the bars to come away," said Grandfather, "he came along and didn't want to be left. When I looked back from the crest of the hill, I could see him driving the stock gently from one shade to another." Grandmother, who had been quiet all this time, said, "I can tell you what's the matter with Old John; he wants to see Homer before he leaves this afternoon for Silverton. I shouldn't wonder but that's it, so you must go over before you start and say good-bye to your old pardner," said Grandma, as she passed the pumpkin pie. "I expect when I see you get into the buggy, I'll feel as bad as old John, and may act just as strange."

I went over alone after dinner to say goodbye to my old friend and tried to cheer him up. I pulled some volunteer oats and took them to give him, also some burnt cookies Grandmother gave me, as he always liked something sweet.

It was as perfect a day as you ever saw, the sky was very high and blue and there was just enough breeze blowing to move the leaves on the trees. As I came to the pasture I was slightly disappointed that Old John wasn't at the bars to meet me. I could see, however, all the stock up under a large spreading oak that stood on top of the small rise we called "Snake Hill." A lark was singing on top of a tree—singing as if the yellow spot on his throat would burst. I didn't see Old John, but saw Old Charley, the yellow horse, standing with his head down. Cattle stood close and more than a hundred sheep stood silently by. Some small lambs were playing on a log near, just as small children might play at a funeral. As I came closer, I saw in the shade of a mighty oak, Old John lying dead. It seemed to be, and undoubtedly was, understood by everybody but the young lambs that there was a funeral in progress. The yellow horse stood partly over him with his nose resting on the dead horse's shoulder. His big brown eyes were open but were not focused on any one particular thing. They were blank and expressionless, but his body was still warm. I sat against the big round

back that had carried me after the sheep so many dark nights and I thought of the picnics we had gone to, and I fondled the mane I used to braid for the gala occasions. I could see the faint scars of the collar and tugs that had been left when years ago, he had helped father clear up the landscape of a pioneer farm. I saw him as my own mother's pet that grew to be the mischievous rogue that got into the pantry and ate up all the pies and drank the milk, and then hid in the back pasture. I saw him in the days my sister Orla rode him to the Fourth of July celebration, where the bass drum and the plug uglies made him prance for miles, and I thought of him as the friend, even the philosopher, the teacher of children, and everything that a perfect horse could be. And it seemed a fitting occasion, if he had to die, to die on such a perfect day, the very kind of a day he used to enjoy most.

I was some time getting away from the scene and when I got to the house and explained the delay, it affected them all, even to the hired man, who didn't like Old John because he got lazy in his old age.

But in the afternoon, we hitched up to go to town where I was to stay. I didn't have any baggage, only a rooster that I had for a pet. Grandmother had been snuffing a lot, since she heard of Old John's death. She said that when I went away to Silverton, she might not see me again, but she went puttering around from one room to another, fixing up something in a bundle. Finally she came to say goodbye and brought a pumpkin pie, a pair of heavy wool socks, and a handkerchief, which I needed right then. When we drove out past the barn where the big Balm of Gilead tree stood, that had been my mother's riding whip once when she rode on Old John, she broke off a branch for me to smell of the sweet fragrant leaves, on the way to Silverton. Grandfather and I ate the pie, we were afraid it would get shaken up and dusty. When we got to town and saw all the folks we made them all sad by telling them of Old John.

We all went down to the store, and it seemed fine to stand behind the counter and play clerk, but as evening came on and Grandfather went home, it didn't seem so good. I didn't see any boys; everything was strange, but our own folks; but it was great to know we were there and we lived there, and to see the farmers' boys come in, and know you were one of the town boys. It seemed like a year to the next week; when I saw Grandfather in town I ran to him and he said, "Your grandma said I should bring you home with me, she wanted you to hunt the eggs for her." I told him to ask Father. So when he got ready to go in the evening, he drove around in the buckboard while I held the horse. I saw them talking in the back part of the store, and heard them say something about its only having been a week; then they laughed; Grandpa came out and said, "Yes."

We drove through the big covered bridge toward the Waldo Hills, five miles. On the way we planned to fool Grandma; I was to get out at the barn and slip along the picket fence, and hide in the yellow rosebush near the gateposts, and I did. So when Grandma came out to open the gate she said to Grandpa, "I thought I told you to bring Homer back with you." As Grandfather drove through, he said, "Yes, but since he went to town last week he is changed, he ain't the same fellow that used to hunt eggs for you; in fact, he didn't want to come; he's got in with the boys there, and he's forgotten us; in fact, I hardly knew him." By this time Grandpa had begun to unhitch the horse and he had overdone it; Grandmother had put her apron over her eyes and her shoulders began to shake, when I dove out of the rosebushes, so it scared the horse, that I forgot wasn't in on the job, and instead of it being a great joke, like Grandfather and myself thought it would be, instead we all broke down and cried. Afterward I went all over the place before dark, gathered all the eggs and found three new nests, and that night we popped corn and ate apples, and

I told them all about Silverton and how strange a place it was. In a few days I went back to town. Then I got better acquainted.

I was big enough to help clerk in the store, but wasn't what you would call a safe clerk. I used to clerk while Father went to dinner. Mrs. Francis, a woman just out of Silverton, used to be a regular customer of ours; she came one day and I sold her a yard of gartering; after that, for a long time she didn't trade with us. Father met her on the street one day and asked her why and she told him. She took from her satchel a small piece of gartering, expecting to meet him she was prepared to explain. She said, "There's what your son sold me for a yard." Father, a thoughtful person, took the gartering, which didn't measure more than ten inches. The two went to the store and found it measured just a yard, if you stretched it to its limit. Mrs. Francis was given some new gartering and some candy to take home to the children, and was soon back on the books again.

Silverton is located on Silver Creek, fifteen miles east of Salem. The stream runs through the middle of the town and is crossed by one of those homelike old covered bridges that bear all the latest posters, social, theatrical and agricultural, including the lost, strayed or stolen. There was every class of people in Silverton but negroes; there were Chinamen, and Indians lived there in small numbers; but, for some strange reason, no coons. The founders of Silverton were all old pioneers that came mostly in 1851, and most of them came from Ohio and Illinois.

No city, no matter what size, could have the glare and good times that the people of Silverton enjoyed. But the main population were highly educated people, and very prosperous, as they are to this day. The population still varies, owing to what's coming off in town.

They had formed a brass band, but it hadn't done very well. They had home talent shows and debating societies, and several lodges and a few saloons, but, above all, Silverton had among its population lots of great characters; men of great learning and wide experience, who spent most of their time playing marbles, and month after month I kept from hard work under the pretext that I was studying the character of the people of a town of three hundred.

My father was, and is now at eighty-three, a man of the highest form of education, a philosopher, a musician, a teacher, and above everything, a man. Considering that we had sacrificed country life for the city, he wanted to take advantage of the few advantages the city afforded that the farm didn't; so I started taking music lessons of "Aunty" McMillan. She wasn't my aunt—no relation—but she was very stout and chunky, and wore curls with a high polish on them, and most always you call that kind "Aunty." She had gotten so stout she couldn't play the difficult pieces any more, those you reach one hand across the other to play. She just taught and told how she used to play. We paid her in fresh milk for the lessons she gave me, so that if I failed as a Paderewski, Father wouldn't be out ready money.

The method she taught was like all really great inventions—it was simple; and I have to smile now when I think that no one thought of it before. It was better perhaps for a transient teacher to teach than one regular in the city—in fact, it took a brave person to buy property and settle down on such a method. The first day I came with a quart of warm milk; that is, I started with a quart of milk, but the sidewalks were very poor in Silverton then. I reached her home and prepared for the lesson. She gave me a sort of a lecture first on music, said that it had come to stay, that it would soon be counted as a part of every first-class education, and that it got easier as one progressed. Then she produced a large music book with the notes all numbered. The keys of her organ were

numbered, and then with an indelible pencil she numbered my finger nails, and I took the stool; and while she counted time with a short smooth pointer—"One, Two, Three, Four," I began to get in touch with the various numbers; and as I was fairly good in numbers up to seven, I progressed so rapidly that after the second lesson she gave me a chance on a reduced course in classical music, which was to come later on. If you got a certain number of these chances it reduced the price half. As we paid in milk it meant for the big set of lessons I would only bring one-half as much as I should have had to do had we bought them.

Father had sold out the store on account of my clerking and was surveying a good deal, and working with deeds and legal papers some. He asked me how I got on at the music

and I simply smiled and showed him the tickets, "Reward of Merit" printed on them, and he was really too proud to enter into a conversation. A few days later I saw him talking with "Aunty" McMillan, and I could see she was praising me, as Father was having trouble with his eyes. He never could bear to hear good said about his children, he was so tender hearted; and I guess the people knew it, because they never told him much. Other people in

Silverton thought I was nothing, because I drew pictures and took music lessons, while the other boys worked, and because Father was so well educated and I was foot in the class and still taller than the rest in the same class; but they never took into account that regardless of height we were of

the same age. Finally "Aunty" McMillan got up a musical concert by her pupils, the proceeds to go to buy a new organ for the church. She played the old organ in the church; she could do that, as it was slow time and plain music. I was to play first in the big musical. I came first on the program, and there's where the error of her life was made, as in coming to the Town Hall after milking the cows I got the numbers that she had put on my nails late in the afternoon wet, and they had blurred and slipped, and I didn't notice it until she led me out and seated me; then she backed into the wings and spoke in low tone, "Watch your nails carefully." It was the first public appearance I ever made. Naturally, a fellow gets a little rattled, and when I looked at my hands, the numbers were most all gone. She yelled, "Look at your nails," so I finally said, "My numbers have slipped," and the audience in general, and my father in particular, wanted to know what the nails had to do with it; in fact, he suggested that I quit looking at my hands and look at the book; so when she explained her new Eastern method, they broke up the meeting, and "Aunty" McMillan left town on the early stage and hasn't been a resident of Silverton since. It was some time before the town got over the musical shock it gave them.

CHAPTER II

THE old brass band hadn't done well and the organization of a new band was talked of around the post-office. The old instruments were brass and had the old-fashioned rotary valves, and the strings kept breaking. The town thought we should have a new band, nickel-plated instruments with the late piston valves. As it would advertise the town, and so long as the band didn't play would give it an up-to-date appearance, the wealthier citizens contributed, but notwithstanding my exhibition and failure at the McMillan musical demonstration, they let me in, and I played the snare drum, because it was the easiest to carry. Our instruments came, and the town nearly went wild over them, and we began practicing every night in the band hall. We got thirty dollars to go and play at ordinary picnics, and you came and got us in a wagon with flags on the side of the box. We played along for a few months this way, and then we thought of uniforms. We wanted something that would distinguish us from the common herd. As it was, unless you carried your horn or drum all day at a picnic, they couldn't tell us from the rest of the farmers, which reflected on the city. So again we levied a tax on the citizens, and some of them moved out of town to escape it, but under the head of education they contributed according to their means, as their property that lay in town would be enhanced in value by the uniforms.

We began to receive large booklets of uniforms, shown on handsome young men with pink cheeks. Ralph Geer was the only member of our band who looked like the lithographs, so after a long discussion we picked out the ones that were on the fellow that looked like Ralph, and ordered seventeen assorted uniforms, second-hand, from Lyon & Healy, of Chicago. They were supposed to be all sizes between such and such. The colored pictures of them showed them to be a beautiful light blue gray, with red stripes down the pants leg, and the coat was a long cutaway, with three rows of big brass buttons on the chest, and large red epaulettes on the shoulders, and a lot of red and gold braid on the coat tails and collars. The caps were high and leaned forward, with a short straight stiff brim and a red plume went in the front and top of the cap.

There wasn't much sleeping done after the money order left town. The whole town sat around the post-office stove and wondered whether they would steal the money order or not, but we kept it as much of a secret as possible the day the money left.

There wasn't a man in town, or a drummer that came to town that could figure accurately how long we would have to wait. After the order had been gone about a week, I hung out at the depot and watched for the train that was due at noon each day, but each day the express messenger said he hadn't seen or heard anything of them. Father finally came to me and said that the whole town thought the reason I hung around the depot was to get the first dive into the uniforms when they came. Of course he knew different. He knew it was because the musical strain ran so strong in our family, but the town in general was about ready to accuse me of crowding, so he said, "You go now out in the hills and I'll let you know when they come." I knew when

I left the depot that it was suicide, but there was nothing else to do, so I went. A few days later I saw a man driving fast over the country road through the hills, and knew it wasn't the doctor's rig—it must be the band uniforms had come; so I left the gap in the fence I was watching for a man and ran to town, and found that they had been there two days; father had been out of town surveying. When the people saw me they left their stores and houses and went

with me to the depot. I asked them if they looked like the pictures, and they said, "Just exactly, only finer." I was astonished to hear that the others had all taken theirs and left only one for me to choose from. I had never seen uniforms, only in catalogues, and once at a circus, and never had had any on except I wore once Father's Good Templar Lodge regalia for a few minutes. They had come in a big box, and this one suit and cap was all that was left in the box. I took it out and held it up against me, and the crowd laughed, while I saw nothing to laugh at. I could see that the man who cut it didn't especially have me in mind, so to pacify the mob I stepped into the trousers, and I think I took one or two more steps before either pants leg moved. This suit they had left for me was cut to fit a man five feet six, that weighed two hundred pounds at least, and who didn't carry much of his weight in broad shoulders. I stood six feet one, and weighed one hundred and thirty-five. I put on the coat, and John Wolfard yelled from the crowd and asked if the epaulettes didn't go on my shoulders. I told him on horn players they did, but on drummers they always folded just across his bosom. The coat tails struck the calves of my legs. Fortunately there was a big fold at the bottom of

the trousers, and much gray cloth that could be taken out of the back of the coat, and with these remedies it got to fit pretty well. All of the pants had to be made over anyway, as they were not spring bottom, which was all the rage then, so we had them cut that way. Of course, our popularity grew quickly with these clothes, and half of the young fellows in the band got married that winter, while the gilt braid was yet new, and before the moth holes that were in most of them got together. Our prices jumped from thirty up to fifty, and you still came and got us, and brought as many of us away from the celebration as you could find.

There was but one Democrat in Silverton, and he was one in every sense of the word. He hadn't said much for years—just paid his bets regularly every four years without much back talk—but that fall when Grover Cleveland was elected for the first time Jake McClaine's voice lasted about half an hour. Then he wrote what he wanted to tell you on a slate. He wrote to the leader that he wanted to defray all of the expenses of the entire band to Portland the next Saturday night, where they were going to give Cleveland a big Democratic rally, and have electric lights. Of course, we accepted, as Jake McClaine had paid more toward the new instruments and uniforms than any other man in town.

We had to leave Silverton at three o'clock Saturday morning, and go in a "dead-ax" wagon twelve miles to Gervais, so as to catch the morning train on the main line of the Southern Pacific. I rode directly over the hind axle and lost the only gold filling I ever had up to that time. We got there at daylight and had

breakfast that had been specially prepared for us, for which Uncle Jake paid. He wasn't an uncle, but like "Aunty" McMillan, was fat, so everybody called him in Silverton, "Uncle Jake." We took the Albany local, and by eight o'clock were in Portland, forty-seven miles from Silverton. It was the first time I was ever there without some one holding me by the wrist, and it seemed great. The uniforms kind of made us brave, and Uncle Jake marched ahead and we played as we marched up the main street, which was First Street. On the bass drum was printed in red letters,

"Silverton Trombone Band," and people would yell "Hurrah for Silverton!" while Uncle Jake would answer them by yelling "Hurrah for Cleveland!" Uncle Jake frequently sold cattle to the butchers there, so before we knew it we had stopped in front of a butcher shop, and were playing while he was in the back end of the shop selling cattle. From one butcher shop to another we went, playing all the time, and many of us marching in new shoes on the first cobblestones we had ever seen. Finally in the afternoon we bought a box of apples for lunch. The day was dark and cloudy. In front of one shop Uncle Jake brought a butcher, who he said had bought more cattle than any of the rest, and he wanted us to play for this man, number eighteen in the new book. Eighteen in the new book was the one piece of classical music which we bought when we got the uniforms. The only difference that it bore to the other quicksteps was that it didn't go quite so fast, and about the middle of the piece it had sixteen bars rest for everybody but the barytone player, and from long and careful training we had reached a stage where we could play up to within a few feet of this sixteen bars' rest and almost all of us stop simultaneously, at which point the barytone player would run a little scale that was called a cadenza, and we would all watch the leader's head and when he nodded we would join in and finish out the piece. It was a pretty thing, and we told Uncle Jake we were holding it for the reviewing stand, where we wanted Cleveland to hear it; so he said all right, he would have the butcher there to hear it also. After marching all afternoon and having our photos taken, the big parade started at eight o'clock.

After marching in the parade until nearly midnight it came our turn to stop and play before the reviewing stand. Most of us were so sleepy we could hardly keep our eyes open, and the horn blowers were a sorry lot. Between their new shoes and their lips, they were about done up. Their upper lips hung out far and were purple. They looked like they had all got into a bee's nest and had been stung on the lips. The leader cautioned each member that the supreme moment of our lives was upon us; that all the other bands were present, and that he thought Cleveland himself was. He said, "Whatever you do, don't play when you get the sixteen bars of rest; and you, there, with the snare drum, don't roll out into that open space as you have always done before." It was an awful moment. Uncle Jake was still to be heard bragging to everybody what a piece it was. Finally,

with the greatest difficulty, the piece was started. I thought I had a pioneer idea that they didn't need me, and for fear of being accused of breaking down the piece in case they made a fizzle of it, I would quit as soon as we got started—and did. I just made motions without hitting the drum; but it wasn't a new thought, as nearly every other member had done the same thing, so when we approached the sixteen bars' rest the only one player was the leader himself, and he had the tremolo stop out. He stopped just as a large sky-rocket went up. We hadn't been used to fireworks—that is, big ones—and the only barytone solo anybody heard was the barytone player yelling to the man next to him, "Look, quick, Tom, at that skyrocket." Uncle Jake directed the butchers he had brought down to hear number eighteen, to the fireworks, and we never resumed the piece, and never saw each other until we met the next day on the train bound

for home. Aside from that one piece the trip was a great musical triumph, and Uncle Jake was the hero.

A few more years passed studying character, when I joined the Good Templars Lodge. Father wanted to retire from it, and I was to take his place. I knew them all on the street, but when my name was voted on and accepted, and the Saturday night I was to take the oath came, it was different. I went all dressed up and was quartered in the outer waiting room. I had heard so much about riding goats, and even Father wouldn't tell me what they did to you there. He didn't even go the night I joined. All he would say was that he didn't want to see it. The outside guard brought me a red and gold regalia and said, "Put it on around your neck." Then I waited some minutes and heard singing in the big lodge room. It was upstairs over the town hall, and no one was every allowed to peep in unless he was a member. Finally I heard raps like a hammer, and people walking. The outside guard, who was one of Uncle Jake McClaine's hired men, came, and I asked him if there was anything to be afraid of. He said he couldn't tell me; that it was against the rules. I noticed he had cloves on his breath. He said, "Get ready; they may call for us any minute." I asked him if I had mussed my hair when I put my regalia on, and he said I had, slightly, and he fixed it, and he gave me some perfume to put on my handkerchief and my coat lapel. Presently a rap came at the door, and a small peep hole opened, and a voice came in bass, "Who's there?" The hired man said something and again the voice at the peep hole said, "Admit him." We were then in another small hall and the guard noticed that every now and then, unless I held my mouth shut, my back teeth chattered. I wasn't cold, quite, but that feeling that, thank heavens, you only have once in a lifetime, was with me. In another moment another queer rap, and a female voice asked, "Who's there?" Uncle Jake's hired man took me by the arm, and said in a strong, bold voice, "A brother wants to enter." The truth was the brother didn't. He was all in, and about out. I heard the female voice say, or rather sing it, that there was a brother outside knocking for admission. Then a great rustling of feet was heard when the lady at the wicket said, "Bring thy brother in." I was past recognizing anybody by this time, although the woman at the door turned out to be our hired girl, but I couldn't recognize her then. They all rose and sang, while I marched to the other end of the great hall and knelt before a throne; and a man with more cloves on his breath and a more elaborate regalia, read something about rum being a serpent, and strong drink was raging. Another rap or two with the mallet, and then we took another circle while they sang, and then we stopped in front of a lesser important booth, and there had more reading, and another odor of cloves. But all this time my neck would pop at any attempt to get easy and relax to anything like a natural pose. Finally I was escorted to a table and sworn, while the mob kept singing. They produced a book; I signed and paid two dollars. Then they escorted me to a seat, and a recess was declared to congratulate the brother. Even then I made an attempt to walk across the floor, and wouldn't have made it without assistance. There we were all chums, but, with the regalia, so changed.

After that about all we did was to buy candy hearts at the post-office that had reading printed on them: "I love you," or "Will you be true?" Sometimes the printing would be too strong for a Good Templar lodge, but if it was we could always sell the one heart for what the whole sack cost. I was later discharged from this high body for sleeping on a billiard table in Portland, to the disgrace of our whole family, and especially, my father.

Easter Sunday to the country boy is about the biggest thing on the boards. Easter itself is a tame day compared with what those of the weeks previous have been. In the far West—and I suppose it's the same all over the country—boys hide their eggs and the lid is temporarily off—that is, you can steal another boy's eggs during the period previous to Easter without its being a crime punishable by parents or law. In fact, you can steal anybody's eggs during the fortnight previous to Easter Sunday, and lucky are those homes where there are enough eggs for breakfast till after the big feast, composed chiefly of eggs, roasted, boiled and parched by the open fire on Easter day.

Sometimes, if a boy makes a bad throw Easter, then nothing but broken eggs follow in the free fight. But among the quieter boys the worst effect is acute indigestion from a mixture of over-done goose, guinea, turkey and hen eggs.

The last big Easter campaign I took part in was in Silverton, and all of us boys in the neighborhood were jealous of Joe Welch because we had a hunch that Joe had the greatest number of eggs. He was the shrewdest of us all, and what was more to the purpose, he was close-mouthed, and there was nothing in his silent laugh at the post-office corner of evenings to tip us off as to just where his eggs were hidden. He had made several big steals from other boys, and it was surmised that it was he who had acquired Warren Libby's collection of turkey eggs.

Late one afternoon, when I had been kept in our house longer than usual by a lesson in arithmetic by my father, and just as I was starting downtown, I went to take a last glance at the place where my eggs were hidden in a hole under the barn, when, lo and behold, there was Joe Welch crawling out from under our barn with my eggs in a sack. Before he saw me I darted back into the house and watched him from the attic window. He looked all around, and then ran out of the barnyard, across the street to his own home and crawled under the house from the back. He was gone for fifteen minutes, and when he came out he brushed his clothes, looked all around, and seeing no one, went downtown, whistling a new tune our brass band had just received from the East. I saw that the day was all mine—I was born under a lucky star—so I ran and got a sack, for I smelled big business. Sack in hand, I crawled under Dr. Welch's house, and away up in the darkest corner, next to the chimney, were the eggs with my own initials on them. There was a big heap altogether, and it seemed as if every egg that any goose, turkey, hen or guinea had laid in the neighborhood of Silverton for the last year was there. I wiped my eyes at first, then my heart began to beat so loudly that I was afraid Mrs. Welch, Joe's mother, would discover me, for I could hear her walking around in the house plainly. I got all the sack would hold comfortably, also filled my hat, and then made a trip to our calf pasture, where I hid them in a fence corner.

I had to make another journey to get them all, for there were goose eggs, turkey eggs and guinea eggs, besides all shades of hen eggs, including some yellow cochin eggs I knew Joe had stolen from another boy. When I reached the fence corner with the last load I got a shock. The fence creaked, and I thought I had been discovered. But it was a false alarm, and I was about as proud as a pirate could be when I realized that no one would ever look in such an out-of-the-way place for the eggs.

That night when I went to the post-office Joe Welch had a twinkle in his eye that no one understood but me, and I let on that I was just as certain as he as to who had the most eggs. But when I saw him the next day he was more thoughtful—he had a far-away look on his face, and I—well, I guess I looked a trifle happier than he did.

I guess it was when I was about seventeen I raised a pup. I liked him more than I did some people and he preferred me to some dogs, so it would seem natural that we were much alike in general character.

I loved him then and I love his memory now. He died in my lap in Portland, Ore., when he was about six years old. Some one had poisoned him. Every time I go to Portland there is no place I look on with more deep regret than the spot near the railroad yards where he lies buried.

I owned this dog's mother and he and I became pals. He was more than a dog. He had almost human intelligence, but passed in a crowd for a dog. In that way he fooled fleas, as they stayed on him in preference to me.

I named him Duff when he was a few weeks old, and when I was at the Lewis and Clark exposition in Portland a long time afterwards many were the people that came, not to see my exhibit of birds and horses, but to talk about Duff. These people had been impressed years before by this rather ordinary looking bull terrier. Like a good many very worthy dogs, he would have been a joke at the New York Dog show.

He was anything the crowd he was with wanted him to be. His early character in Silverton represented the local color of the town. As a result he was more or less a clown. He and I went about without much purpose, and where there was the least resistance—not meaning that we tried any of the doorknobs. But we sort of loitered around at our leisure, and in that way got to know each other very well, and incidentally a lot of other people.

One Sunday we went to Wilhoit Springs, a mountain resort, where many prominent people came from Portland to spend a week or so. The proprietor was a cross, surly man, and his guests were pining for something intellectual. They soon found Duff. They marveled at his tricks and his keen mind. They said they wished he was the proprietor of the soda springs.

It was here that Duff introduced me into the first real artistic atmosphere I had experienced. The man that admired my dog chum most was a lithographer named Walling. I drew pictures for him on bark and chips while Duff was resting. Mr. Walling told me that both of us ought to come to Portland, where he was sure our talents would make a hit.

We finally did go to Portland after several years, and Duff's friends received us warmly. I had expected to make my fortune and to support Duff royally. But my drawing was not appreciated in Portland as it was in Silverton.

The first money I ever acquired from art was brought in by Duff. I got him a position at the Standard theatre, where he joined the song and dance team of Hickey and Clifford. They paid me $1.50 per week for the stunts Duff did every evening during their few months' engagement.

One rehearsal was all the dog needed. I doubt if any chorus girl's vanity ever took her to the theatre with more regularity than this dog's pride in his act took him. His part was, at a given signal, to run on the stage and grab Hickey by a prepared pad concealed under the actor's coat tails. Then Duff was swung around and around hanging by his teeth.

I sat in a front seat every night and applauded. Sometimes Duff would come to the footlights and peek over at me and wag his tail. He turned a few hand springs and jumped rope and never objected as to who came on first. This made him the most popular actor with the stage director.

In Silverton, before we went to Portland, Duff did more tricks than I could tell you of in a day's talk. He carried in stove wood; he rode up on the hay fork holding to a sack; he sat on the cowcatcher of the locomotive; he was the retriever, the bird dog, the shepherd, the clown. He could catch a coin or a baseball that was laid on the top of his nose. He would turn a back somersault just for the asking. What is more, he understood any plain language, the kind we used in Silverton.

When I was an engine wiper he was the watchdog of all the company's property. Thus, when Receiver Scott, of the O. R. Co., doubted the dog's ability to watch the engine all night as he slept on the cab seat—where I ought to have been, but was accustomed to stay away from my post and sleep in my bed—Duff attacked the inquisitive receiver who had sneaked up in the dark, and treed him on an old-fashioned pump in the yard of a nearby hotel.

A lady once, when I was boasting of Duff's wonderful intelligence, said:

"Do you mean to tell me that I can't hide your knife where he can't find it?"

"Yes," I said; "it would be impossible."

I told Duff to go in the next room till we hid the knife. She put it up on the top shelf of the sideboard, behind the only real cut glass there was in Silverton.

Duff came in and began to sniff with his head up. Before either of us had time to stop him he mounted the sideboard, knocking down all the glass and breaking it and brought us the knife.

An actor finally offered me $100 for Duff. My father came to Portland to see me about accepting the offer. We talked it over one day on the Stark street ferry. Duff was with us and we thought he knew what we were talking about. He looked as sad as father, and I felt I couldn't bear to sell him, though I couldn't imagine anything that one hundred dollars wouldn't buy.

Father said life was made up of such sorrows and dis-appointments; that while nothing could be finer than to spend a lifetime with a dog of such wonderful intelligence and sympathy, still a hundred dollars at compound interest at 10 per cent. For twenty years would buy so-and-so and so-and-so, and that in the professional life Duff was leading he might be stolen.

I was about to agree. All this time Duff had stood between us, his eyes on the floor. I spoke to him and he raised his head slowly and looked at father full in the eye.

In that look he saved us. Father turned to me and said: "Homer, I guess we can't sell him."

At that Duff leaped high in the air, bumped father's hat off his head, caught it in the air and ran frisking about the boat with it.

No, he couldn't be sold; there was something in Duff that showed in his eyes and prohibited a price.

The Silverton *Appeal* was the one newspaper in Silverton. It was a weekly, that the editor told me might some time be changed to a daily, if the town ever responded to its encouragement; but the town didn't respond, so that the Silverton *Appeal* is still a weekly. For a time it got to look like it would be a monthly. The editor always set type and smoked long stem pipes; with big shears he culled from every other paper. Lots of times he took cord wood for subscriptions, and, after that system had been inaugurated for a few years, he ran a wood yard in connection with the Silverton *Appeal*.

The *Appeal* was unique in its way; there was an individuality about the paper that one would know it was published in Silverton and nowhere else. The editor was about as smart as any man in town, but once in a while he got things into the paper that they didn't see till they were printed. I noticed an advertisement once for a lost horse that read as follows: "Found, a bay horse fifteen and a half hands high, left hind foot white, small star in the forehead; any one describing the property, and paying for this advertisement, can have the same by calling at my farm."

There was one strong opposition to the Silverton *Appeal,* and it was a hard competitor. It was the old covered bridge that crossed Silver Creek, on Main Street. Sometimes the old bridge had more news on it than the *Appeal;* people got so they posted some of the town scandals, and it always had more local news than the home paper. H. G. Guild, who was the best editor the Silverton *Appeal* ever had, was shrewd enough Saturday nights, before the *Appeal* appeared on the streets, to go out and quietly tear down some of the big headlines that the bridge had and the *Appeal* didn't, and in that way the *Appeal* finally got ahead.

The job work in connection with the Silverton *Appeal* was advertised all over the bridge, and throughout the *Appeal* the job work was as queer as the editorial page. One advertisement announced a sale of Ai Coolidge, the banker. It appears that Uncle Ai had got overstocked with old harrows and a mixture of livestock, and was going to sell them at auction. The advertisement listed among the enumerated stock "one two-year-old yearling bull."

Of course, it wasn't the intention of the Silverton *Appeal* to compete with any other paper, and, as the editor started the wood yard for subscriptions, after that had run a couple of years it was frequently remarked that he had got to be a better judge of cord wood than he was of news.

But the people of Silverton appreciated the Silverton *Appeal;* they many times remarked that they liked it lots better than the Portland *Oregonian,* as it always had more home news in it.

I used to drift around into the shoe shop. Simeral was a ball player, so he used to sit in his shop and talk over the errors of the latest games. If you have ever sat in a shoe-maker's chair, you are bound to admit that it is the most comfortable seat you ever fell into. I used to sit there and whittle leather and talk with the shoemaker; I must have whittled leather scraps for two or three years without miss-ing much time. Finally one day by mistake I cut into an upper that was to be made into a shoe and it nearly broke up the shop; I couldn't pay for it, and we didn't want to ask Father to settle, so I joined the firm to get out of it.

My only duty then in town was to get up our cows that we let run in the streets nights, hoping they would find some neighbor's garden gate open. I used to get them up and milk them, but going into this firm as a shoemaker was such a big surprise.

I told all the young men around town and some of the old ones that thought I drew too many pictures; in fact, I told a few girls that thought because I did not have pocket change enough to take them to dances, that I wasn't much. I went home early, didn't tell Father, because he didn't want me to work; just wanted me to study faces and draw.

I didn't sleep much; turned and tossed until four o'clock, then got up and went to Simeral's shop. I thought of the cows, but didn't get them up; in fact, didn't have time and didn't think it would look dignified. Simeral came about nine, and let me in, and before he had the key out of the door I was into a roll of red morocco, starting on some boots that would have sold even before they had been finished. He came to me and said, "Homer, there ain't a boot in this shop I would trust you with now, but I saw a feller

the other day with two and when he brings them in they're yours. In the meantime, I have twenty cords of wood up in the alley next to my house. If you will go up and saw that twice in two and toss it up into the woodshed, by the time that's done there'll be some boots in."

Of course I saw the peculiar part of learning the shoe-making trade, but I had told so many people that I had to go. I had been sawing wood about half an hour, just long enough to be thoroughly disgusted with any branch of the shoemaking trade, when I heard a familiar cow bell, looked around, and saw my old father come driving our cows past this very woodpile. There was no way to escape, as they were too close. I thought of many ways of eluding discovery; perhaps the safest of the many would be to bend over and saw wood, knowing that as he had never seen me in that position, he would likely pass on by.

But the older and shrewder of the three cows recognized me and stopped, perhaps because she saw so much of her milk on my boots. I didn't look up, but kept on sawing, pulled the hat down tighter and felt strange. I also felt Father's hand on my shoulders and dreaded for once to tell him the truth, as it sometimes hurts. He said, "Homer, will you please tell me what has happened? Have you had any trouble at home? Speak up plainly." "No," I said, "nothing wrong there." "Then tell me what this strange departure means. I got up early, called you, and you were not in your room. Tell me just the plain truth."

"Well, I'm here learning the shoemaker's trade of Frank Simeral, and I started in to saw." "You're what?" said Father. "I'm learning the shoemaker's trade." He made me repeat it till it sounded ghastly, then taking me by one hand he squeezed it gently and affectionately when he said, "Homer, look me square in the eye." I thought on that particular occasion just a stab over the shoulder would do, but he said, "No, right in the eye. You know, don't you, that I sold the most beautiful farm you or any one else ever saw, mainly that you might live here in Silverton so that if by any chance you didn't turn out to be a cartoonist, you couldn't say that I hadn't done all that was in my power to do for your art education. You know that, don't you?" "Yes," I said. "Then do you think you are playing me fair? Mind you, I am delighted to see you learn this trade, but don't you think you ought to have had the manhood to come home and learn it of me? I've got twice as much wood as this to saw."

CHAPTER III

ALTHOUGH Silverton was situated in a great hunting country and had lots of good shots, I never took much to hunting, perhaps because I was a poor wing shot and deer were too pretty to kill; but I had heard of the great flocks of geese and ducks out on the coast of Nestucca, so I went over to have a great hunt, and the first day I was there I actually

found a band of geese big enough so that when I shot into the entire bunch one on the outskirts fell. When this small goose hit the sand, he raised to his feet and ran, me after him, and after quite a run I overtook him and found only one wing broken. I always had wanted to own live wild birds and things, so I saw my chance. I carried him to the cabin carefully and cut up a cigar box lid into splints and set his

wing and I was overjoyed to see an expression in his cute little black eyes that he sort o' knew I was trying to cure him instead o' kill him. He got rapidly better and I started for Silverton with him and there astonished our family by the kindly way this Hutchins goose let me doctor his wing. Father helped me doctor him some and finally when we took the splints off his wing, his affection showed more than ever, and to tell the truth he and I grew to be the nearest and dearest friends possible, not being of the same species. He used to follow me all over the place, and once when I was sitting down by him in the barnyard he brought me some straws, evidently wanting me to build a nest. He was a great talker and an alarmist; he would come to me after I had been away downtown and try his best to tell me what had been going on in the barnyard while I had been away.

In fact, he was my real chum. When I came into the barnyard mornings when the frost was on the ground, he would greet me all smiles, as much as a goose could smile, then he would step up on

one of my boots, which was quite an effort, and hold his other foot up in his feathers to warm it, and if I started to move he would chatter and cackle that peculiar note of the Hutchins geese, as much as to say, "Hold on, don't move, I'll tell you another story." Meanwhile he would warm his other foot.

When I went for a walk in the back pasture, he would walk with me at my side, just as a dog would do. There he spied a slight knoll and he went and stood on it erect, as much as to say, "I'll watch out for hunters while you eat grass in peace and comfort." When I had finished my pretext at eating grass I went and stood on the knoll, and as long as I stood there he fed with perfect confidence that I was watching out for his welfare, but when I walked away he ran to me chattering something good naturedly, perhaps telling me that he had not finished. We really had great times together, but finally spring was approaching and I had noticed how he could fly around the barnyard. Father came to me one day and warned me that if I wanted to keep that goose I had better clip his wings, but he said, "I hope you won't. You say that you love animals; now show it by letting this goose alone, then when his kind come by in a few weeks going north for the breeding season, he will join them and be happier than he is here."

I replied that "of course an outsider might think he would leave, but in reality he would not. The goose and I

have talked it over and he don't care
for anything better than I am, so he
ain't goin' away."

"Well," said father, "when I see
you two together I think as much,
but when you go downtown loiter-
ing around with people that aren't
half as smart as this goose, it's then
that he misses you, and it's on that

account that I wish you would leave his wings the way they
are now. But because after he is gone you will feel bad and
mope around for a few days, I thought I would tell you now
that when spring comes he will leave you, notwithstanding
the bond of friendship, so if you want him kept here (which
I hope you don't) you had better cut the feathers on one
wing."

I didn't want to mutilate his feathers so I left them on.
A few weeks later coming from one of those important trips
downtown, they told me at the house that my pet had gone.
I said, "I guess not." I didn't want to let on that I was
alarmed, but when they were not looking I made some big
strides for the barnyard, and it was actually as still as death.
I whistled but no sound, save an echo, came in return.

I noticed the leaves hung silent on our trees, though the
neighbors' trees were in action. I went back of the barn
and called, but the call was wasted on a few old hens that
"didn't belong." I tried to ginger up some life into the landscape by throwing a few old potatoes at things, but the
brakes were set in general on everything and I went into the
house and found all the family sitting in front of an empty

fireplace with long faces. No one spoke and the only noise was the clock, which ticked louder than ever. It was about dark when father arose and said it was for the best, that "here in Silverton there were no opportunities for him, in fact no pond for him to swim in even, and when you were away downtown, no one that he apparently loved, and if you will think of it a moment, it would have been cruel for you, a lover of animals, to have kept him here all of his life." But there were no answers, just long breaths now and then, until it was time to light a candle. Then the world took on a brighter aspect.

In a few days I recovered with the rest and the long, beautiful spring came. No rain to speak of, and it was fine. I never saw so many picnics and never went with so many pretty girls, and ball games ran all through the summer and the jolliest threshing crews you ever heard of. Fall came and I was hauling wood into the barnyard one day when I heard wild geese; lots of them had been passing over for a week past, on their way south for the winter, but presently, just over the cone of the barn, came some large bird. I thought at first it was a condor; he lit in the barnyard and I was astonished that it was a wild goose. Our rooster hit him and he rose and circled and again lit twenty feet from me. I yelled for the neighbor who kept guns and one ran over, resting his gun on the fence and shot him, while I held fast to the team. It was great to think of killing game right in your own barnyard. I ran to pick him up, when father who was in the orchard yelled at me not to touch him. I said, "We have killed a goose in the barnyard, a wild goose." "No," said he, "don't handle him; I want to feel of your head first to see if you have any bump of memory." Father said, "Do you see that band of geese flying in a circle next to the hill? You used to tell me you could understand this little goose's language and could talk some of it. If you remember any of it now, go out there as near as they will let you approach them and tell them they need not wait for their friend; he is never coming back."

By this time I had realized all. I could recognize his every feature, even to the little black, glossy, soft eyes, which were now half open. Father asked if I saw what had happened, and said, "I'll tell you, as I believe you are too dumb to comprehend. Your friend that used to be has brought that band of geese five hundred or a thousand miles out of their beaten course that he might bring them here to show them where a lover of birds and things treated him so well. They likely objected, but he persuaded and finally they have obeyed, and he left them there at a safe distance and came to see you, and so perhaps renew his love, and there he lies; and if you never commit another murder I hope this one will punish you to your grave. Some murders can be explained to the dead one's relatives, but you can never explain this one and I want to show you his right wing. I think it was that one that we used to treat."

I didn't want to see his wing, but father was determined, and as he lifted the feathers at the middle joint, we saw a scar, a knot in the bone where it had healed.

Everybody is a criminal more or less, and some of the crimes are done by stupid people. Thus I console myself in a way over the death of the Hutchins goose, that perhaps I am a murderer through stupidity and not by premeditation.

John Wolfard, who kept and still keeps the big store in Silverton, had an old hairless terrier dog. I can't remember when he wasn't "Old Bob." He wasn't like other dogs much, perhaps on account of being hairless. The rest of the dogs hardly recognized him as even a distant relative, but he was. No telling what breed he was and I never remember hearing where he came from, but that doesn't matter; he was a terror

after cats, and some time during his life he evidently overtook one that left his or her mark on one of his eyeballs; though it must have been when Bob was young, as in later life he only waddled after them and never got near enough to make a cat more than spit; but the cat evidence on his eyeball was plain to be seen. That was perhaps why he was always trying to wipe out the old grudge. As he got very old, he got to be a painful sight to everybody but himself. He had curvature of the spine, so that his hindquarters got to a place about the same time as his forefeet did, and that impediment, with the full scratched eye that wouldn't close, made Bob an unpleasant sight, and even the Wolfard family that was large cut him socially, as did most all others. He was short tailed and so fat that it made him pant with his tongue out to wag his tail, but somehow or other he always wagged at me, notwithstanding the effort.

It was winter and raining hard one night about eight-thirty, when I was in Wolfard's store. John Wolfard was huddling around the store dreading to make the dash for home. We were talking about the opportunities of Silverton in general, when he said, "The trouble ain't with Silverton; it's with you boys. There ain't any of you got any enterprise. For instance, there is old Bob. I don't want to kill him and still he ought to be put out of his misery, and I have offered any of you boys time and again all the crackers and sardines you can eat if Bob disappears. All I want to know is that he is gone and gone for good, and I don't want to hear the particulars."

I looked down by my chair, and there he sat oily and fat, as sleek as a seal. I looked over behind the counter where they kept the sardines and they looked pretty good. I got up and sorter stretched, when John Wolfard, lighting a new cigar, said, "It's enterprise that you boys lack, the town's all right."

I went into the back part of the store where they kept the bacon and a certain portion of the eggs that are brought to a general store, and the cooking butter. Old Bob was peeking around the chair leg when I said "Rats," and in a second he came grunting through the door, trying as best he could, for a dog that had to walk sideways, to be spry. I went to lift up a big empty coffee sack and old Bob dove into it hunting some rats that weren't there. I thought at the time it was his last rat hunt, but it wasn't. I pulled up my sack and Bob grunted louder as he rolled to the bottom of it. I turned up my coat collar and outside I found a brick they used to block the warehouse door open with. I put that in with him gently and tied the sack and walked across the wet sidewalks to the big bridge. Silver Creek was about as high as it ever got; saw logs were running thick and few animals besides ducks or beavers could have swam it. I felt uneasy, still I felt that it was enterprise, and that while Bob didn't know it, I was doing him and the town a favor. So I stood on the first approach of the bridge and swung the heavy sack over the perpendicular bank, next which the main current of the stream ran. I thought I heard above the roar of the mountain torrent a grunt, then a sickening kind of a splash, and it was just after the splash that I felt dreadful and blamed John Wolfard. The dark night then frightened me and I ran into the warm store, and as I approached the stove I said to the proprietor who was there alone, "Open some sardines and dig out some crackers and put in a few sweet ones for such a job as this."

"Now, remember," said Wolfard, "I don't want to know what's happened." He opened some old sardines. I never have seen the same pictures on cans since, and he brought cheese as well as crackers, and while I ate we listened to the pattering rain. A stranger or two from the streets came and all commented on the high way I was living. John was smoking extra heavy and the whole back part of the store was so thick with smoke that you had to shove it away to

get room to breathe. I had been eating about fifteen minutes when I heard a licking sound on the floor by my chair. Looking down I saw old Bob there licking himself dry. We all saw it at the same time, and the first thought that struck me was to quicken the pace of eating so fast that when John wanted an explanation I was choked on a big square sweet cracker. There was but one solution and that was that he hit the bottom of the creek so hard that he busted the sack and that by some miracle he was washed on the bank at a point where he could get out, and all this done before he strangled, as old Bob couldn't have swam out of Silver Creek during the low water of summer, let alone the high water of winter. I didn't have money to pay for what I had eaten and the friendly way Bob stuck so close to me I did not want to show any more enterprise, so I had to

work the next day in J. Wolfard Co.'s shingle shed piling shingles to pay for a meal that wasn't on the regular bill of fare. Old Bob strangely spent the whole day with me, spryer than he had been for years, and after that night he seemed to pin his faith to me and whenever I was downtown he was always with me when I sat down. He always got right in front of me when he wasn't in my lap and looked intently into my face as much as to say: "When all

others fail me, I can always count on you." Mile after mile
he followed me over the poor board sidewalk until one day
he just died of old age. But as John Wolfard said, "Homer,
as you wasn't around, he died leaning towards a cat."

Silverton was a queer place socially; while the towns-
people were all of one set and there was little of any class
hatred, the rich seldom ever lined up against the poor. Still
if a very beautiful girl came to town all of us boys sort of
took it for granted that she would turn us down if we did
attempt to take her any place, so no one ever gave her the
opportunity. We admired her and talked of her at the swimming holes and in fact everywhere we met, but no one ever
had the nerve to approach her with a proposal of a "Let's
go to the dance, or the party or the entertainment." We
started to several times, but every time we got close enough
to smell the beautiful odor of perfumery our nerve always
went back on us, and as a result she wasn't kept out nights
much. For a long time the girls in town had been about the
same in looks varying according to who had the colds.

One day a beauty came to town to live with some relatives of hers and she pined some time before she was taken
out. I had been out with a threshing crew and we moved on
Saturday to a field near Silverton. The grain wasn't quite ripe
enough, so we laid off until Monday,—an awful thing to do
in that country, giving us all a chance to go into town and
get shaved up and a clean shirt. When I got to town there
was a lot of talk on the streets of a dance to be given that
night at Egan's Hop House out in the Waldo Hills. After my
shave and hair cut it seemed a shame to waste it; that I'd
better go to the dance. My financial condition wasn't what

you'd call very steady. It rose and fell so that I couldn't hardly count on one girl regularly. But I started in where the most affection lay and met a rather sad refusal. She said she would rather have gone with me, but I hadn't asked her since early spring, so she was engaged to go with Harvey Allen, the leader of the Trombone Band. I went down the line and got eleven "mittens," as we called them. Then I even asked one young girl that had never been to a dance alone, and her mother refused, although the girl was willing, so I called it off and went up home and helped around the barn. I waved my hat to the girls I had asked as they drove by in livery rigs with other fellows, and after they had all gotten out of town I went down to the post-office to get the Silverton *Appeal,* when who should I meet but the belle of the village, as we all called her among ourselves. She smiled and I smiled, and she asked why I wasn't at the dance. "What dance?" said I. "At Egan's Hop House," she replied. "Everybody in town has gone but us." When she said the word "us" I saw a new world. The old post-office seemed like the Congressional Library, the plain glass jars full of striped stick candy began to look like

Tiffany's window; the tobacco smoke from the post-office had the odor of beautiful roses, and I started to speak but my jaws set. She said several things that I didn't comprehend, and when I came to I heard her say, "Somehow no one asks me to go to places and I should like to go so well." I steadied myself by taking hold of the fence, as we had started to walk up the street, and I said that I was afraid there was no more livery rigs, and she said, with the sweetest voice you ever heard, a voice that is still ringing, "Can't you get your father's old horse and buggy?" "Oh," I said, "yes, but that ain't good enough." "Good enough," she said, "I thought it was too good and that's why you never asked me to go in it." It was now dark and we were nearly opposite our house. Old Don, the horse, was in the calf pasture and the old-fashioned high buggy stood under the wagon shed where it was sometimes for months without being used. So we agreed to slip out to the dance and surprise them. I told her I didn't care much for such things owing to the crowd that went, but that now I could see a dance as I never had before. So I helped Nettie into the buggy just where it stood and she sat there thinking, perhaps, while I went to get the horse. And you bet I wasn't gone long, and the way we saluted each other when I returned with the horse showed that we had already begun to get chummy, and how much better it sounded than to be distant. I backed the horse into the shafts and harnessed and hitched him right where he stood, but I got half of his harness backwards. I couldn't think of anything pertaining to harness, so when I got into the buggy I drove out through the barnyard as quiet as possible and feeling about as good as a young man ever feels. I was afraid to breathe for fear my arm would touch hers. I wanted to get to the dance as quickly as possible before anybody left so that the advertisement I would get from being seen with this beautiful girl would be as big as possible. I didn't have time to get any candy hearts, or in fact anything, and the perfume she had on seemed a fit emblem to celebrate the occasion. We talked about the weather first, and then how backward Silverton was, and by that time we were out of town and I let the horse

trot. Presently we ran over some rough spot and the old sorrel horse snorted and tried to run away. It was new actions for him, so I got out and tried to find what was the matter. The harness was all right but his eyes were blazing with fire that I could even see in the night. We wondered why he snorted and I got back into the vehicle and we again started on a trot. Finally as we struck another rock, the horse bolted and between his snorts we thought we heard a fluttering.

I finally got him stopped and I put my arm around Nettie before I thought to see if her cloak was in the wheel, but it wasn't. Again I went over the harness and felt to see if the crooper was all right. We couldn't account for it; the only evidence we had was that the horse never started until we ran over a rock or some rough object. So we started again and a few yards when we struck a chuck hole away went the horse and I hung onto the lines; then we discovered what we had done and it was amusing, as chickens always had queered me. Father had compelled me some weeks before to clip my game chickens' wings so they couldn't roost on the back of the buggy seat. In my joy at leaving the barn I had forgotten that my chickens did roost on the hind axle of the buggy, and as we drove out we took the hen roost also, so that naturally when we went over a rock or rough place with the hind wheel, we dislodged all or most of the chickens and they would catch by their necks and flutter back on the axle; thus they frightened the horse that never even shied before at anything; so when I said to the handsomest girl in Silverton, "It's chickens roosting on the hind axle," she exclaimed, "No wonder; I never saw you before to-night without a chicken, and there they are really here with us now." I thought we had lost some, as there were some missing. I didn't know what to do as the dance would soon be over. We couldn't leave them beside the road for fear of skunks or minks. She thought we ought to leave the chickens, but I didn't, as one of our best old hens was in the party and it seemed a crime to expose them to next to certain death. If it had been daylight and I could have seen the beautiful girl perhaps I would have done differently, but we turned around and started back home slowly, as the tired hens breathed heavily on the back axle. We were still sitting as far apart as the buggy seat would let us; had no outward signs of getting closer, in fact we were getting farther apart. She thought young men shouldn't think so much of chickens, while I thought they were next to human. We planned another ride without chickens, but it was the passing of my short reign and I didn't know it until it was too late. That opportunity that the late John J. Ingalls wrote of was there, but not to wait; and when it went it came no more. We got home, but I had hurt her feelings for chickens, and we parted without much friction. I stayed up until the other folks got home from the dance. They were all more or less happy, especially those on the back seats. I told them I had been riding around all night with the belle of Silverton, but all they did was to laugh and especially the girls that had given me the mitten.

CHAPTER IV

I WAS in Portland some time later—was there for quite a while, watching the sights of a growing town. One day a fellow with overalls and a bucket of paste asked me if I wanted to work for a ticket. I said, "Yes," quick. He said, "All right, carry this bucket while I bill the town for Clara Morris and I will give you two tickets for the show." I asked him what it was and he said "Camille." It would be two weeks before the show got there, so I took the tickets after a hard, sticky day's work and went back to Silverton. I exhibited the tickets in the post-office showcase. They were the first Portland theatre tickets ever seen there. I asked a few people what "Camille" was like, but nobody seemed to know. Finally one of my sisters that was going on the other ticket said she knew it was a comic opera and we went to see Clara Morris in "Camille" without a handkerchief and as a result we both had bad colds into the next month. Country people never use handkerchiefs for but one purpose and that is a cold, and as we were free from colds at that time we didn't think of taking any. Oh, I have seen some people use them to dust their hats after the hippodrome races after a circus, but it is seldom they are carried unless they are really needed. So sister and I went without any. We had good seats, the third row in the balcony. We said to each other when we got there—it was a matinee—that we bet it was a good show for every seat was taken. It started off kinder quiet for an opera and without music, which we thought was strange, but about the middle of the first act the main lady fell head over heels in love with a fine, big, strapping fellow and it was fine to watch. Presently some old man showed up, the father of the young man, and it appears that Clara Morris had been in love before somewhere and that seemed to spoil the game. About this time we got to snuffling some and finally Adda broke down and cried aloud, and as she came by me I broke down too. I

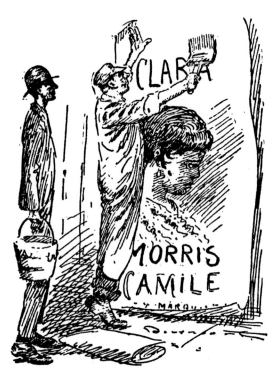

know it must have been bad for other people near us, for some of them got out and left, but we wept right on just the same, and it is awkward crying in the theatre without a handkerchief. I tried to check it between the first and second acts while the orchestra was playing and I told sister that I thought the old man with white hair would finally let them marry; but she sobbed and said in a loud voice she didn't believe he would, as he looked determined. It was awful; our tears were all over us, in fact our feet were getting damp from them. We broke heavier in each act, till the father of the fine looking man she wanted to marry asked her, if she really loved his son, to prove it by promising never to see him again, and at that Adda collapsed completely and neither of us could make a sound. I turned one of my coat pockets wrong side out and tried to use it, when Clara Morris died just as the curtain went down, but we had caught colds from our feet wet from our own tears. Adda's waist, which was green surah silk of the country pattern, looked like isinglass in a new stove. After we left the theatre we met a friend a few blocks away who asked what had happened to us and Adda broke down and began to sob. The friend thought at first that I had beaten her, till I told him we had been to see Clara Morris play "Camille." We got home the next day, looking and feeling bad. The folks asked us how it was and we told them it was fine, but it wasn't a comic opera.

The Narrow Gauge Railroad finally came to Silverton and then the town took a boom toward the depot. I got a job as engine wiper and owing to father's prominence got promoted to fireman on the oldest engine on the road. The other engine was new and shiny and could run faster, and on that engine my father's pioneer friend's son was the engineer and his fireman was a halfbreed Indian. I worked hard for some months and dreamed nights of this halfbreed's bringing me orders telling me to take his fine engine with John Palmer, but month after month it only proved to be a dream. As it was I had given up hope of ever getting away from this rusty old freight engine. But one day at East-Side Junction, a small passing station, one of the happiest days of my life overtook me. Our old train was the first in and we were on the siding. I was watching this fine new Baldwin engine as she came rolling along through Howell's Prairie. She glistened in the sun like a new plug hat. When she stopped I noticed Frank, the halfbreed, shake hands with John Palmer, the engineer, and before I could make out what was the matter Frank was walking over to our engine with some clothes under his arm and a piece of yellow tissue paper in his other hand. He was sullen and looked as though he were more than half Indian. He handed me the slip of paper and said gruffly, "Well, you wanted that engine for a long time, go and take it." I read the paper which was brief, but right to the point; it simply said, "Davenport, fire for Palmer on No. 8." I went over and as I got close to the fine new locomotive it looked even finer than it had in my dreams. Mr. Palmer didn't let on that he was glad until we got out of sight of the Indian, then we had a great reunion. This new engine only burned about half as much wood as the other old freight engine, so there wasn't much to do but sit up in the seat and ring the bell at road crossings and look at streaks of the finest country in the whole world and watch the grouse and china pheasants fly off of the track. We got along fine and I kept No. 8 looking as good as the Indian had her. Our only trouble was that so many boys knew me in Silverton, that every time we went up the mill switch after a box car of flour, as this was a mixed train, these chums of mine used to climb into the cab. Now there is a certain dignity that engineers and even firemen have that is spoiled if everybody comes piling into the cab, especially if women come with small brats, which they sometimes did. This worried Mr. Palmer a lot and made me fairly ashamed. The worst one to climb in was a friend of mine named Jap Libby. We were about the same age, only he had the most nerve, and the mill switch was so rough we couldn't run fast enough on it to keep the farmers from stepping on. Jap Libby not only got on, but then complained about the way we ran the engine. He asked Mr. Palmer why he didn't pull her wide open and let her tear down through the town, at which Mr. Palmer would frown. We always hated to see Jap come worse than anyone else, as he knew the rules were to keep out of the cab. Still he didn't mind them; so Mr. Palmer and I had smiles for one whole trip when we heard one day that Jap Libby had left town for good to go over to Tacoma to work with some Chinamen on a tunnel. A few days later we heard they had an accident and many Chinamen were killed and Jap Libby was hurt. This accident was plainly the fault of the company and they were anxious to settle. Jap was foxy and when they came to the hospital he told them he had no desire to break the company, that he was a railroad fireman and if they gave him a good job when he got well he would call it square; so they signed papers to that effect. He was out in about a week and was firing on an extra freight run. The engineer told him to drop the damper soon after he reported the first morning, and Jap looked up about the steam gauge until the engineer showed him where and after a brief discussion between the two, Jap confessed that he had never fired before. But the engineer liked his nerve so he kept him. He fired about six weeks and was given an extra engine to run. So heavy was the wheat crop in the upper country that within a year Jap was running a yard engine in a Tacoma yard; a most important position. They had a yard speed limit in Tacoma when Jap hit town, but none afterward. He switched cars at forty miles an hour and never broke a draw head, though he did break a few links. There was nothing for the other four engines to do, so they laid them off and the news went all over the country. The officials of the road came and saw from the high bluffs the work of this phenomenon below. The yard master complained and the officials said he hadn't hurt anything. "Keep out of the way and let him run. He is doing the work of four engines and crews." It was true he used up a car load of sand each day on the track as he approached cars, but cars were never kicked as he was kicking them. Combinationfly switches had never been invented in other yards that he was using. The oldest and toughest freight brakeman jumped out of his cab every day though he never cracked a bumper. In fact, children could have coupled them for him. He made combination switches that curled some people's hair, but his stayed straight. Papers wrote editorials about him and cheap actors made puns on him at the vaudeville shows. When Mr. Palmer heard of Jap's popularity he said, "Just wait and give him time." When my vacation came I went to Tacoma just to see his work and though he didn't know where the steam got into the cylinders or where it got out, he certainly put up the hottest game in the railroad way anyone ever saw. His duty in the morning was to follow the overland up, through the long yard to the upper depot and if the traffic was not heavy there he would hitch on to the rear coach and haul her back, but the last time Jap hitched on there wasn't anything to come back. One foggy morning he thought the passenger had time to get up so he was just clipping along about "forty-five per," laughing with his brakeman and his fireman, watching the thick fog part and go on either side of his engine, when all at once he saw the rear of a Pullman. The train had stopped for something and the flagman hadn't gone back. It didn't give Jap as long as he would like to have had to make up his mind. He shut off, reversed and pulled her wide open and then jumped out the window. They were on a high trestle at the time. The engine went through two cars before it thought of starting back, then it pulled out sticking to the track. It fairly howled as it tore down through the Tacoma yards with its broken whistle and smokestack. They had changed some switches behind them and one was on a track that had a fine line of observation coaches that were waiting for the summer trade. It didn't do much to them; there wasn't enough left of them to tell whether they were made at Dover, N. J., or Pullman, Ill. From there she went across the turn table into the roundhouse and out through the brick walls into the Puget Sound where she cooled down, and they are still figuring on the cost of the trip. As for Jap himself, on the fall he got mixed badly and lost an arm and a leg by compound fractures. His men escaped with less injury but it didn't stop him; he got a tricycle that he lives on, and in Tacoma you will see the sign—it's popular with the railroad men—it reads, "Jap Libby, Railroad Cigar Store."

A long spell passed and we didn't do much in Silverton outside of enjoying each other and discussing neighbors. The town got to making improvements after months of public speaking and debates. We finally got a city water works, and it seemed we used to use the hose nearly all the time. I washed the streets from morning till it was too

dark to see the stream. We caused a few runaways, but that had to be expected; we couldn't stay oldfashioned just to suit the farmers with shy teams. Silverton had most everything from a Good Templar's lodge to a bank. The bankers in Silverton were rather unusual as they didn't look like the bankers at Salem. And the fact of Jake McClaine in that banking firm made the name of Coolidge & McClaine, Bankers, the greatest banking institution in the world by a big wide margin; that is, if you count all the deeds that bankers do, both in and out of the bank. They were poor young men when they stopped their covered wagons on the banks of a stream called Silver Creek, and began to look around for better country. They made a few short rides around the valley and mountains, but they came back and finally settled and called the settlement Silverton, and finally people stopped there and took corner lots without crowding. These men were great workers and knew the art of saving. They bought the first crop of calves in their neighborhood and kept them until they grew up, and then sold them for big prices. They got hold of a set of burrs and started a grist mill. They opened a store, they looked at business opportunities from the same focus and in a few years they had actually loaned money. There were many strange parts of their partnership but the strangest part was that the men were so different, yet they got on so well. They were as different, as night and day. Ai Coolidge was the elder and likely the greater money-maker of the two, but he didn't get as much out of life as his partner though he had lived many years longer. Ai Coolidge never made any bad bargains, never took much counterfeit money or never took many chances. Never even gave himself many vacations, other than now and then a camping trip or a horseback ride into the mountains to salt the cattle. On those trips he whittled at a piece of jerked venison and enjoyed life as much as it was ever intended he should. His perfect wife was happiness enough for a man to enjoy and likely in her company he found full value, but his sympathies were never played on like those of Jake McClaine. The two partners must have ridden horseback half of their lives, though it wasn't a range country. They figured interest on horseback, though they never kept a book of the firm's business, which was rather unique; but they soon began to acquire farms, as they loaned money from ten per cent up and they enjoyed giving the closest attention to those farms. I used to ride with them on a pony and sometimes behind one or the other on the same horse, and I have seen them ride for hours without saying a word to each other. They each had a dog and each found fault with the other's dog. Jake McClaine had a keen sense of humor and he continually exercised it on his more thoughtful partner. One day when we were at the Spooner place, Jake kept yelling at Ai's dog. Every moment or two Jake would yell in a clear voice, that echoed in Drift Creek Cañon, "Here, come back!" then turning to his partner, he'd say, "Ai, why don't you make that dog come back?" Ai rode along, never paying the slightest attention. Strangely enough, each dog would obey his master, but wouldn't pay any attention to the orders of the other. Finally Ai's dog chased a steer for ten minutes and Jake cursed and called, but the dog kept on. Finally McClaine turned to Ai, demanded that he make his dog mind; whereupon, with a twinkle in his eye, Coolidge said, "I'll give him to you, you make him mind." Coolidge's dog had been caught in a steel trap when he was a small pup and had one toe missing on a forefoot. The dog would travel all day on three legs and did, all the balance of his life, except when he saw a squirrel, then he seemed to forget all about his once sore foot and ran like any other dog, and this was an opportunity for Jake McClaine, as he would argue with his silent partner for fifteen minutes at a time why Coolidge didn't make his dog walk on four legs, instead of three, whether there were any squirrels in sight or not. But I think Coolidge rather enjoyed Uncle Jake as a clown, as he rode miles without ever making a reply to any of his talk. Jake

McClaine had a bay mare and she and his shepherd dog Prince were steady companions during that middle portion of life and early latter portion that is so important to all mankind. Jake McClaine made the best chief marshal at the Fourth of July parade of anybody around; in fact, you put a red or blue sash around him and he looked like a Greek god. His beard hung in ringlets like ancient Homer's; his clothes were worn with the most artistic careless swing

imaginable, but there was something more to Jake McClaine than artistically hung clothes, something more than any other banker in the world. True, he would take advantage of you in money matters the same as other bankers; he would squeeze money till it got slick and shiny and to avoid argument I can say that he had perhaps all the small business ways of great financiers; but there was another side to him, another Jake McClaine, who lived in the same house with the banker, and with that Jake McClaine there were no partners, and nobody ever asked to be his partner. Few, if any, were capable. I never saw a funeral pass through Silverton that Jake McClaine didn't ride his bay mare at the head of the procession, and I heard of one passing through town where he rode at the head that I was unfortunate enough not to see. They were the only times he ever grew very serious; no one ever died in the vicinity but what Jake McClaine was there when they needed help. If they were poor or rich or just well to do, he took complete charge; made the arrangements for the funeral and rode ahead and let down the gaps in the rail fences and whether the funeral was over a fellow pioneer or someone's hired man, with bare head, with his white curly hair and beard, he looked as fine a type of just plain man as you ever saw. I never saw him look worried only once at the graveyard, and that was the first year the band tried to play at Decoration Day exercises. The graveyard hadn't been running long and there was only one soldier buried there, but the G. A. R. wanted to remember him, so the band and Uncle Jake went there with the big parade just as if the graveyard was full of soldiers. Jake rode the bay mare ahead of the procession as usual. Part of the band lived in the country and didn't get into town to practice as much as they should. We had just got some new music and among it was a funeral dirge, the first ever brought out there. It was No. 21 in the new book. The country members were late getting in and the big rush and the few stiff beards at the barber shop put them still later getting to the band hall, where the procession was to form and march to the church. They came finally, out of breath, and we were half an hour late, so we went to the church on double quick march, backed up to the church solemnly and started for the graveyard down below town. No. 21 in the old book happened to be our favorite quick-step, so when the leader yelled No. 21, the town members turned to the dirge and the countries turned to the quick-step. We had been playing about half a mile when I noticed there was something wrong; we didn't just seem to swing right. It was hard for some of the old soldiers to keep step. At the graveyard there was a big crowd waiting and me play-ing the snare drum, which was muffled in black. I could look around, and I saw by the expression of Jake McClaine's face that there was something wrong. We were game, though, and played right up until we surrounded the grave, and stopped. There were two bass players, one from town and one from the hills, and they made a peculiar contrast. Nobody mentioned it, but the joke was out and an old soldier with a wooden leg said to Jake, "No wonder I couldn't keep step, when I used to in the army without any trouble." Jake McClaine said to him in a low voice, "Keep step! I nearly fell off my mare."

The average winter weather of Oregon is very rainy, while as a rule the cold is not the most severe by any means. But the worst night I ever saw, I saw in Silverton. Father and I were sitting by the fire listening to a tearing and howling storm one night about nine o'clock. We were feeling comfortable as we knew all of our stock, which wasn't large, were in under comfortable sheds. We were getting ready for bed, and wondering whether the storm would tear the chimney off the house or not, when I heard a slam of our barn door. I knew if father heard it he would make me go out and fasten it, notwithstanding the storm, which had me completely cowed, but father wasn't afraid of the dark howling nights and I knew it, so about every time I thought the door would slam, and I had it pretty well timed, I would clear up my throat and was stalling it off in fine shape, till father engaged me in a conversation by asking me what was the matter with my throat anyway, and when I went to tell him the door slammed, and sure enough he heard it. His eyes sparkled as he straightened up in his chair alert. "There, Homer, that's the barn door, and as awful as this storm is, we must get out to the barn and tie it shut, or this wind will tear it off its hinges in less than an hour. And what's more, such a storm as this might tear the roof off the barn, if it gets under it. It's the worst storm I have ever seen in Oregon." There was nothing to do but put on all the rubber clothes we could find, tie them, and take a lantern and start for the barn, some fifty yards from the house.

We held on to each other for protection, the light going out with almost the first awful crash of the storm. We hung on to each other for dear life, and bunted against a turkey and some chickens. They had been blown out of the trees where they were roosting, and were groping about on the ground. We reached the barn, got inside and stood for a moment almost exhausted, and drenched to the skin.

We noticed that there wasn't a light streak anywhere in the sky. We relit the lantern, for it was as black as pitch, and the roar of the storm as it tore past was something awful to hear. It had that effect that night air and rain sometimes have of making the brave fear. It was just the night that would cause the bravest of men to shudder and quiver like a leaf. We got hold of the slamming upstairs barn door, and held it fast as it slammed shut with the noise of a cannon. After tying it safely, we delayed before starting back to the house. We wished our bed and dry clothes were there in the barn so that we could stay all night. We looked at the cows and horses, all showing fear, as they listened to the storm. We were so cold we had to start.

We couldn't make a mad dash, because in the fury of the storm and the absolute blackness of the night, we couldn't keep our bearings and were liable to hit a tree. Father suggested that we go back through the barnyard to the street, then hold to the fence along the sidewalk to the house, which we did. Through some miracle the lantern stayed lit.

We had just reached the sidewalk and were feeling our way toward the house, when a dog came into the dim glow of the lantern and shook himself. It was old Prince, Jake McClaine's dog. "That's strange," said father, "as he is never away from Jake."

Just at that moment through a lull of the noise of the dreadful night, Jake McClaine yelled at us. We couldn't see him although he was as near as he could ride the bay mare, owing to the four-foot walk. We yelled, "Where have you been?" He said in return he had been to Salem to see Bush (the banker there). "Drove out," said he; "got back at dark, was wet through anyway and my hired man said that over town they believed the Hults up near Cedar Camp were all down with diphtheria. And I got to thinking maybe they needed help, so I had the mare saddled and I am going up."

"Jake," my father called, "are you crazy? Have you lost your wits entirely? Don't you know that when you get into the live timber in the mountains you will be struck every twenty feet by flying limbs?"

"Well," he said, "I have thought of that, but there is no way to get around that belt of live timber, and I thought as I couldn't see at all, I might take a chance and dodge the best I can, so I'll be off."

"Jake, hold on." But no answer came from the black night but the howling storm. We even waited a moment till the sheets of water seemed to shift till we could call again, but no answer, and we got into the house. Father held me by the wet hand, and looked me in the eyes with the expression of a wild man for fully a minute. We didn't speak; then he said, "Homer, I wonder if you realize what a night this is, and what a man such a man is." We got off our wet rubbers and coats and bundles and sat at the warm oak fire till nearly two o'clock, talking of Jake McClaine. We thought of him in this way: he with Ai Coolidge, have the best houses in all Silverton, the finest, softest beds, with the biggest and best

pillows; he has the best things to eat; the warmest fireplace: he doesn't need to work, yet he would leave all that to go twenty miles into the mountains through an eighth-mile strip of big timber, off into the dead timber, to investigate into the health of just a family of poor mountain people that didn't know enough to move to the valley, just because the man wanted to live like the trapper and hunter that he was. It was a trip that all the money in the world couldn't have hired me to make.

But this wasn't all that gave us food for talk; as father says: "It was this same Jake McClaine, this man with unkempt hair and beard, with one pant leg in his boot and the other out, that came when my family was down to death's level with smallpox, when we lived in the hills; when neighbors, yes, even relatives, had fled and left me alone; when no one came near to help me, then this man that we yelled to in the storm, came unsolicited and came every day and stood to the windward side of the house and asked after my needs. But," said father again, "I would have done that for him, although smallpox in those days was looked upon as death itself. But I wouldn't go with Jake to-night if he gave me all of his money. Common sense wouldn't permit me to go into those mountains to-night. It's only a few hours till morning, then I'd go, but not to-night, no siree! I owe too much to my own family."

We really hated to go to bed, it was such a pleasure to have such a strong character so forcibly impressed upon our minds. Morning came, the poor landscape looked bewildered; it had been through an awful night. The trees were resting, they hadn't had much sleep and they looked tired and worn out. The streams were out of their banks, and we heard of some bridges that were gone, down on the prairie.

We were afraid we would hear that Jake's body had been found. We went over to see his wife to see if his horse had come home, and his family were naturally as much worried as we, though no news had come from him. That afternoon

Jake came from the mountains; he had reached there just at daybreak, he said. No one was stirring around the log cabin; said he called but no one came. He finally went in and found them all sick and in bed. Hult asked him to see about the children over a few beds away from his. He said, "I ain't got them to answer since yesterday some time. And they ain't none of them taken their medicine lately."

Jake was looking them over when he slowly took his hat off. He found that out of the large family, four of the children were dead, so he came to town after coffins and medicine, and was soon on the way back with the doctor. Then next day he came as a funeral all by himself; he had hitched his mare in with Hult's mule, and as he passed through town with four small coffins in the vehicle on his way to the graveyard, most everybody joined him and went with him. Those were the times when Jake McClaine didn't have a partner, no matter how many firms he was in.

CHAPTER V

SOME time after I quit railroading, I was working in a field, through which the railroad track ran on father's farm just below Silverton. I was plowing this piece for the first time. Father came down and looked on while I plowed a couple of rounds; he said to see me plow put him in mind of an old sow that they used to own in Ohio. I asked him why I reminded him of a pig, especially at plowing; he said the similarity was this, that a sow could root up a field as well as I could plow it.

Each day when the train came through, my friend Palmer, the engineer, would throw me the daily *Oregonian*, which he had finished reading.

After receiving this paper, the work would be lighter during the balance of the day and it eventually prolonged the plowing until spring came, and about the only crop we had was old papers. While reading through one of the papers I noticed a paragraph saying that a car would leave Portland, Oregon, on Wednesday night of the following week—this was Friday—for New Orleans, with a select aggregation of sporting men from Portland to the Dempsey-Fitzsimmons championship fight. I read the statement many times, and felt more enthusiastic after each reading; so I went to the barn with the team, told father it was too dry to plow, and took the next train for Portland.

When I got to Portland, I went to the publisher of the *Sunday Mercury*, as it was the only sporting paper there; told him I was an artist and wanted to go to the big fight at New Orleans and do him a series of pictures. He asked me how much I would charge him, and I told him all I wanted was my transportation for the round trip. Ben Walton was an enterprising man, and strange as it may seem, agreed without ever asking to see any of my art work, and that fact alone made it possible for me to go. When I found I was really going, I wrote to my relatives and friends at Silverton of the great trip I was going to take, and in a couple of days my grandmother sent me by express a basket of roast chickens, a half-dozen pies and cakes, some hard-boiled eggs, and an assortment of pickles, as a light lunch to eat on the train.

I was not certain just where New Orleans was and as the day approached when I should leave, I became very nervous, owing to the fact that I didn't have a dollar to start on the trip with. I hinted so strongly though, the day I left, that the publisher of the *Mercury*, determined to make the experiment a success, gave me ten dollars. He had had a banner painted that I was to present to Dempsey as he came from the ring victorious. In getting the transportation, he was unable to get it further than Fort Worth, Texas, and return; but the railroad official, who was T. W. Lee, afterward general passenger agent of the Lackawanna Railroad, told me the railroad company would have the balance of the transportation for me when I reached Fort Worth, Texas, which they didn't. Wednesday night the train started over the Union Pacific Railroad, and the carload of sports advertised in advance, had dwindled down to one, myself, and such a tame looking sport that the company decided they hadn't better send a special car, so I sat up in the smoker and tried to look wise.

At Denver we had coupled on our train a carload of real live sports, most of them being from San Francisco. I remember finishing the lunch the day we left Denver, and when we got into New Mexico we struck a blizzard, and the block system stopped us for three days, two days of which we had no food. And I might say at this point that real sports are not good humored when a train is up to its sides in snow, especially when the buffet is empty. My memory was that I had hurried over the lunch I had brought from Oregon, so I looked through the train and found it in the smoking car under the seat. I invited the man with the biggest diamonds to have a bite with me, and as we struck the carcasses of the chickens and got them warmed up again, we went over them and over them with much care and comfort.

Finally a snow plow came to us and we proceeded slowly, arriving at Fort Worth, Texas, Tuesday evening, and the fight was set for the next night, and as the regular train would not get there in time, the car of sports paid out $22 each, making up $500 for a special. Mr. Frank Maskey, the candy man of San Francisco, he of the large diamond, who had appreciated my invitation to lunch after a fast of two days, paid for me, and we sped on at the rate of a mile a minute and reached New Orleans in time.

I put up with the rest of them at the St. Charles Hotel, and at night went to the fight with a letter for admission from the editor of the *Mercury.*

I can describe the fight briefly by saying that owing to Fitzsimmon's roughness and general coarse bringing up, I never had an occasion to even unwrap the banner that cost

$150. So the next day I traded it off to a colored boy for an alligator, thinking at the time I would exhibit the alligator at the small towns on the road the following season. 'Twas the first one I had ever seen and I thought they were worth a great deal of money until next day the chambermaid in the St. Charles Hotel told me they cost thirty cents.

The next evening in the hotel lobby, Billy Vice of San Francisco came up to me and said, "Here is your $22; I got the railroad company to refund the money, as we paid them for the special and it was their fault the blizzard struck us"; and besides it wouldn't be fair, as he says he told them most of us were newspaper men. It was like another blizzard striking me, as I was in the act of asking Vice for a quarter to get something to eat, but $22 put me on Canal Street right, mingling with the sports from every town in the Union. I hadn't gone far when I heard the cluck of a chicken. I turned quickly and saw a nigger with two sacks, one in each hand. I overtook him and asked him if they were game chickens; he said they were. I then made known to him that I was the greatest game chicken fancier that ever set a hen, and it was my intention to purchase a choice lot before returning to Oregon, which was to be in two or three days. He took me to his home, where I examined several. I asked him his price and it appears he saw me counting my money, as he told me that being I was a visitor to New Orleans, I could have the two roosters for $22. After a sigh, I accepted. I took one under each arm and proceeded to the St. Charles.

I had no place to put them, just had to stand and hold them. As it was late at night and I had my key in my pocket, I managed to get to my room without being detected. Once in my room, I was compelled to remain in the dark, as to strike a light meant a cock fight that would arouse everybody. So I set one rooster on the back of a chair and the other on the rack made to hold the towel, which stood by the washbowl and pitcher, and with as little noise as possible I went to bed. Before I fell asleep I thought of the next morning, which was fast approaching; I was afraid they might crow. I had apparently just closed my eyes when I was startled by a loud clapping of wings, and a shrill crow which seemed to echo in every room in the hotel. At the same instant the one that had been roosting on the chair back, flew full tilt to the one that had challenged, and before I could spring from the bed they were fighting on top of the washstand.

It was just getting gray in the morning and the room was barely light, but once together the feathers flew, and before I could reach them they had knocked down the water pitcher. I finally grabbed and held one rooster, while the other one treed me on the bed. I was in the most awful position a fellow could be placed in in a strange hotel, with a Spanish gamecock in my arm treed on top of the bed, with the other rooster strutting around over the broken pitcher, just dying to get a bill hold of my bare shins. I pressed the button and soon the bellboy came, but he couldn't get in as I had left the key in the door on the inside. I tried to explain my position over the transom. After shivering about for an hour, I thought of the only scheme of letting them fight until I dressed. Then I took them to a back street and there proceeded to hold them until the afternoon, when hunger drove me back to the hotel. The colored chambermaid found a bucket and a tub and I put one under each and never felt such relief in my life.

I was getting pretty hungry and I was completely broke save for twenty cents which I invested where it would mean the most in oyster soup. All at once it dawned upon me that I was five hundred miles from where my railroad trans-portation was available, and that I had a hotel bill yet to pay, and like a fool had paid out my last dollar for two of the spunkiest gamecocks I ever saw. One of them would keep a man busy, while two kept me up night and day, and threatened me with insanity, or something worse. I happened to recall that my friend the publisher, as the train pulled out of Portland, had yelled to me something like this: "If you get broke down there, draw on me." So I went to a bank and told the cashier I wanted to draw on Ben Watson of Portland, Oregon, for $50. "Well," said the cashier, "where is your identification?" "Who?" I said. "Where are your letters of credit; who identifies you?" "Oh, no one; I don't know anyone in New Orleans but Jack Dempsey, and he is confined to his room." All of my friends, the sports, had left for home while I was walking the back streets with a rooster under each arm.

"Well," said the cashier, "why don't you draw on him for $500? It will be just as easy as drawing on him for $50, if you don't know anyone here, and have no letters of credit, not even a letter of introduction; I'd draw on him for $5,000, if I could find a cashier that was right. The best thing you can do is to step out of line and go outside and draw a big full breath." I said, "What can I do, I am broke." "Who are you and what do you do? You are evidently not a banker." "No," I said, "I am an artist sent here from Oregon. Came to illustrate the Dempsey-Fitzsimmons fight, and I want to get back home with my pictures. The man in Portland told me if I got broke to draw on him, so that is why I have come to the bank."

I then remembered I had a letter of recommendation from Sylvester Pennoyer, at that time governor of the State of Oregon, and known to the world at large as Grover Cleveland's particular friend. I let the cashier look at the letter, which said that my father was an honest man and a good and loyal citizen, and that he hoped I would turn out as well. The cashier said that if my father were there he could get money on the letter, but he seemed to take an interest in me and somehow guessed that I hadn't traveled much. I told him this was the first trip and the last I would ever take. He put on his hat and took me next door to the managing editor of one of the leading local papers, who, he said, was a great believer in Governor Pennoyer, and that was my only chance for getting any money. I showed the editor Governor Pennoyer's letter and told him I was almost starving in a great city like New Orleans. The editor looked thoughtfully for a moment, more thoughtful than editors generally look, then he handed me a blank draft and asked me if I would fill it out.

I took the pen, asked him the day of the month and I think the year; he told me and then there was a long pause. I had to tell him that I couldn't fill it out. He laughed and said, "Young man, you just saved your bacon. If you had filled in that, I wouldn't have paid a cent. But," he said, "I'll take a chance for fifty." So the editor filled it out and I signed it and he endorsed it, and the bank cashier paid me $50.

I felt so thankful that I offered to give the editor one of the roosters that I had at the St. Charles, but he declined with thanks. I bade him an affectionate good-bye and in five hours was aboard the train for Portland, Oregon, with an alligator, two gamecocks and sketches of a championship fight, and in five days was in Portland with the sketches and game chickens, but no alligator. The alligator, when we got to Denver, where it was twenty below zero, refused to move even a toe, so thinking him frozen stiff and dead, I tried to bend him and he broke in two like a brittle stick, and I threw the pieces out the window. The truth is that had I put him in warm water, in five minutes he would have been swimming, but I wasn't as much on alligators as I was on roosters.

I got home to Silverton and told my father of the great things I had seen, the glorious time I had had, but father seemed to be worried about something that didn't please him; his face bore an expression of disappointment. I asked him what was the matter. He said he was disappointed to see me come home with only two roosters!

The roller-skate craze hit Silverton just as the spring-bottom pants fad was leaving town. It's funny how fashions vary. I remember one spell in Silverton that we were having our trousers cut with so much spring on the bottom that only the end of our toes were exposed and six months after that high tide of spring-bottom pants we wore trousers legs so tight that it was difficult for some of us to get our feet

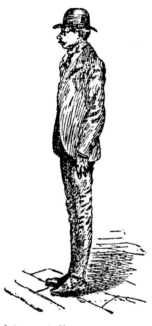

through them, and it was at the beginning of the tight-pants craze that a fellow with a curled moustache and a pocket knife with a girl's picture in it and fifty pairs of roller skates came to Silverton.

He started a skating rink in one of the big vacant halls on Main Street, and the first week there was standing room only. The second week about half the skates were in the shops for repairs and several of the town's best citizens had hard work to straighten up. The proprietor of the skating rink made a big hit socially. He wore a new brand of perfumery and refused to give the receipt, so there was no competing with him along that line. The bottoms of his trousers were not any bigger than the tops of his shoes, so he had those of us who wanted to follow fashion killed at that junction; but a few of us got busy with the local tailor and we run him pretty close on tight pants. Some of us had to grease our insteps and heels to get into them; but the brand of perfume he wore, aside of the bottle he had, was evidently distinct and extinct, and owing to that fact he was the envy of the town.

This skating rink had a queer effect on the town in a general way; it acted as a sort of a leveler, an equalizer of station and fashion. The well-to-do skated with the poor, the handsome with the homely, and the freckled with the fair. It was one general mix-up in which there were no favorites. The

funniest part of it was to stand across the street and listen
on Saturday afternoon. Above

the noise of the town was this
general local roar of the skates,
and as if periods or punctuations,
the building shook with dull
thuds. Sometimes they fell in
clusters, others, one at a time; but
you didn't have to wait long to
hear two or three dull sounding
whacks that made the windows
rattle on the upper story of the
building.

    I took two or three short dashes
at it morning and evenings before

I went to work, but they proved unsatisfactory. So I decided to wait until the next Saturday afternoon, when there were going to be some prizes given. I went early that afternoon, fairly groomed for the occasion; I felt fit like a trained athlete. I rented a pair of No. 10½s and went to work; had been going about an hour, when the world seemed pretty serious; in fact, I had fallen so often that it had ceased to be a joke. My hair was slightly mussed on the back of my head and I had seen about half a

dozen quick flashes of fire, when I thought there must be some easier method. I took a leave of absence for half an hour and went over to Tuggle's place (he was the biggest bellied man in town) and borrowed a pair of his overalls. My stepmother had sort of an economic pillow, just one pillow that went clear across the bed, so in that way you saved one pillow slip. With that pillow and Mr. Tuggle's breeches, I remember turning in the rink door with a broad grin. I could see before I put on the skates that

I had the game beaten, and it was going to be fun, too, as the biggest crowd was there that had ever been in attendance, and they were getting pretty reckless.

I lowered the pillow into the seat of the overalls after I had put them on, and then got a boy to hold the pillow up against my back while I put my vest over it, and I dove out into the thick of them. To my astonishment and a little to my disgust, I didn't fall. I leaned back and tried to fall once to see how it would be, and I really couldn't. I'd been skating fifteen minutes when I did fall, but fell forward and slammed my hands on the floor.

In a few minutes I fell again forward and slammed my hands again. By this time that too had ceased to be a joke, as the ends of my fingers were throbbing as if they had hearts in them, and they were getting heavy to lug around, when an elderly lady, who had had some troubles of her own that afternoon, skated up to me and told me she thought perhaps we went at it too fast; so we were leaning against the wall talking over the scientific points of it, when I gave the audience a rare treat.

While leaning there talking, all at once my feet, that were close together, started and rolled out toward the middle of the room.

I don't think I bent a finger, but I fell exactly like a tree, and, lo and behold! the pillow burst. It must have been five minutes before they got through laughing all over the house and the better skaters were having great fun swinging through this "goose hair." In a few minutes the feathers were so thick you could hardly see, and they followed in a

boiling streak after every skater. Finally the largest girl on the floor, Lizzie Mescher, inhaled a feather, and she began to cough so that the people living in the outskirts of the city lifted up the windows and listened. We all thought it was a joke at first, until we saw she was black in the face. The strongest men in the crowd were beating her on the back and rather luckily for her, though unluckily for me, she finally coughed up the feather, which hit and broke one of the biggest window panes in town, so great was the velocity with which she let go of it. She didn't skate that afternoon any more; she was big and stout when she got hold of the feather, but after she had wrestled with it for five seconds, it took a blacksmith on each side of her to steady her while they got her out of the building. It was a good thing, in a way, as it acted as a warning, so that those who still skated kept one hand over their noses and mouths; but the proprietor of the rink was afraid they might break more window panes, so he declared a recess of ten minutes while they swept out the hall, and at this point came another big laugh, as after three men had been sweeping twenty minutes they hadn't got over three feathers out into the street, while a wagon load remained in the hall. Some fellow who had been used to sweeping out stores yelled to sprinkle them, so they did; but they only quelled the big feathers, which amounted to about half of them, while the dangerous kind were all up in the air and wouldn't come down to be sprinkled, so they had to close the rink for the afternoon—what had started as the busiest afternoon of the season.

The proprietor of the rink tried to collect damages from father, and I think there was a compromise made. But the skating rink had one moral effect upon the people of Silverton that it might never have had, as the town was full of philosophers, mathematicians and smart men, and none of them would have believed if they hadn't seen it, that just a little wet feather could break a pane of glass.

The next Fourth of July Silverton was down on the bulletin boards for a celebration, and as in all small country towns on such occasions, the village was keyed up to its highest pitch. Long before noon our barnyard had commenced to fill with wagons and hacks belonging to friends and relatives and a few people we owed, and among the wagons I recognized that of father's brother, Uncle Ben, who lived up in the Waldo Hills. When Uncle Ben came to town, he always put his team in our barn and came into the house to joke and talk business, and though he was full brother to my father, Uncle never ate with us for the simple reason that my father ate plain food, while Uncle Ben

didn't care to waste any time with anything but fancy cooking. His wife, Aunt Lou, was about the best cook in all that part of the country, and I suppose Uncle Ben had gotten used to eating her cooking and couldn't stand for anybody else's; in fact, it was Uncle Ben's pride and pleasure on state occasions to invite any dignitaries of the day to eat of Aunt Lou's lunch, and if they knew Uncle Ben's family at all well, they always accepted, as the meal was one you would seldom forget.

On this occasion Uncle Ben drove into the barnyard, and from the wagon in the heat of the sun he removed the gorgeous lunch that his wife had been two weeks preparing and carried it into our wagon shed. There it lay quietly hid under the seat of our old buggy, which stood there year after year, seldom being used other than that the chickens roosted on the back axle. I had been downtown early and had hunted up my friend Bob Patton, the undisputed champion sprinter of the county. We searched in vain for a foot race, but every sprinter was shy, and I, as his manager, saw that the day was going and we would get no race, so I suggested that we take his saddle horse and hitch to our old buggy and drive to Marquam, a village of about forty inhabitants, not counting the town cows, some eight miles below town, where they were also having a celebration. "All right," said Bob; so we proceeded.

We left Silverton about eleven o'clock and neglected to get anything to eat as our minds were too much on business and on the way to Marquam, I, as trainer and manager, suggested that we should have had something to eat but that now we had better postpone it until after we had run the race, if we got any. We arrived at Marquam, hitched our horse among the trees, and circulated among the farmers rather shyly, suggesting now and then in mild tones, a foot race. All of the athletic young men seemed to have heard of Patton and were not willing to run. Finally we found an old farmer who said he had never been beaten, and he would not allow any city chap to bluff him, so after half an hour's effort on my part as manager, we made the match: one hundred yards, judges on the start and finish, start at the drop of the hat.

We placed all our money, after great difficulty and then began preparations for the race. The farmer was first to show at the start; he had tied his suspenders around his

waist tightly, so that they gave him the appearance of being gaunt. He had dampened his long beard, that it might not catch too much wind. He had removed his boots, and was going to run in his sock feet; his pants legs having been wound around his legs and the socks pulled up over them, giving him a very athletic appearance. Patton came a minute later with his regulation suit on, spiked shoes and even corks to hold in his hands. We could have collected the money then and we blamed ourselves afterward for not doing it, as the farmer that was going to run and his backers all had stage fright, and they delayed going to the post, trying to get up some excuse to quit; but we preferred to run it out in true sportsmanlike manner.

After a couple of attempts, the hat fell and they were off, and in half a minute I was actually blushing. The old man had beaten Bob fifteen feet, the judges at the finish said, and when judges from the start came up, they said the city chap had five feet the better in the start. I thought they would knock my head and shoulders off, so great was their excitement. Bob used as an excuse that a dog had got in front of him, but that only added to the humiliation, as the dog outran him further than the farmer. We gave up the stakes and made a bee-line for the buggy, crestfallen and broke.

CHAPTER VI

THE hunger that had been hidden by the excitement of the race soon came to the surface again, increased tenfold, and we were fairly bent over with hunger and pain. Bob asked me to go among my friends and hint that we were broke and had had no dinner. I did, but it seemed we had lost our friends with the race.

I returned to the vehicle and told Bob we had better drive to Silverton as fast as possible, where we could get something to eat. We hitched up and were preparing to start home when, in the act of putting away the halter, which the horse had worn coming down, but which I was now taking off and putting under the seat, my hand ran against a cool surface and glanced off.

I looked under the seat-curtain and saw a sight that I didn't soon forget. It was an enormous dishpan of high polish, the contents of which were concealed by a clean linen tablecloth over the top. I lifted the cloth, and could perceive that it was a most bountiful dinner. I felt faint and weak and grabbed the buggy wheel. Then I called Patton, and when he looked, his countenance changed from that of the humiliated athlete to that of a victor. We thought it belonged to someone on the ground, so we lost no time in driving away with it.

We drove for a mile and a half to where the country road crossed, by way of an old, covered bridge, a beautiful stream called Butte Creek. We halted at the side of the stream, and there spread out this royal lunch. 'Twas the most luxurious affair I have ever seen. There was fully enough for twenty people,—six roast chickens, the most sumptuous pies and cakes imaginable; biscuits buttered, some with preserves between, others with slices of cheese and pickles, and there were several loaves of salt rising bread. There were tarts and cookies, sliced tongue, pickled pigs' feet, radishes, and about ten dozen hard-boiled eggs. We spread it all out on a grassy peninsula, and proceeded to devour it until we fell into a stupor. We ate until our hands and feet went to sleep.

It was with the greatest difficulty that we mastered sufficient energy to pack up the remaining carcasses and uncut pies and cakes and the general debris that would follow such a meeting.

We drove into Silverton, taking our time. As we approached town we met people coming away that yelled and asked us how Ben's lunch was. Some of the blood by that time had got back to our brains, and we were able to understand why the horse pulled so heavily on the way to Marquam. When we got into town we heard wild stories over the abduction of Ben Davenport's lunch, and that Ben had been on the warpath, and that it was a good thing for us he had gone home, as he had invited the orator of the day, the chief marshal, and a man that was running for Congress, to dine with him, and they had accepted.

All hands had proceeded to our barnyard, where they expected to spread this great lunch underneath a pear-tree in the back yard; but, to their astonishment, they found the buggy wherein he had carefully concealed his treasure gone, no one knew where. Ben had gone to my father and threatened to divide the family, but father knew nothing of it. He thought possibly I had discovered the lunch under the buggy seat, and had taken that as an excuse to leave the country, and in his own heart felt much relieved; but Ben was furious. When I met father he wanted me to explain at once, and I did, as I have in this story, and I think he believed me. But the less I can say about Uncle Ben the better.

I might add, however, that though he and Patton live in the same neighborhood, they have never been seen sitting on the railfence talking, as sometimes neighbors do. The truth is, they haven't spoken since. The ablest debater couldn't make Ben Davenport believe that we didn't know the lunch was under the buggy seat when we drove out of town.

Uncle Ben was a genius in a way; he was what you would call a success. If he owned a good pocketknife with a good rivet that he could snap the blade back and forth from his finger to his thumb, then if he had an old knife that looked good but wasn't, to trade on, then he was happy.

In some trade he once got a gib bay horse with peculiarly heavy feet. He was about the finest looking horse anybody ever saw. He was sixteen and a half hands high, and as well made as they could be put up. But there was one mistake about him,—he evidently wasn't intended to work, and if you got him to move after you put a collar on him, you would have to haul him.

It was a lucky thing for Ben Davenport that he got hold of the bay horse, as most all of the property that he accumulated afterward was directly or indirectly due to the big bay horse. Everybody that came into that part of the country owned him at least a day, and he put several gypsy camps out of business. Whenever a stranger came over the road, Uncle Ben had occasion to go out with the big bay; and unless the man knew the horse he couldn't resist giving everything he had for him, and a little to boot. After he was traded off, Uncle always came to the family with a smile and said: "Well, I have done great business today. I've got rid of old Broadfoot." All of our family would plead with him to stay rid of him. He'd promise never to get him back again; but inside of twenty-four hours, he came with just as broad a smile and said, "Well, I've got back the big bay." And it was through that kind of operations, the rake-off, as it were, that went to the kitty, that Uncle Ben got a good financial start. He traded and retraded the horse for years. Every time he passed out he was called "Old Broadfoot," and every time he came back he was the "Big Bay."

Silverton kept growing more and more, and traveling men with bigger diamonds began to come to town. I drew pictures for lots of the drummers, and several of them told me they sent to Paris every few months to buy the goods they sold in Silverton. They said that in Paris most everybody drew pictures, and that some day they'd take me. I told father about their promise to take me to Paris, but he only smiled.

It seemed that I ought to be doing something. I was getting pretty big for my age, and still there didn't seem to be

anything that I was just suited for. Finally, McMahan's circus came,—a one-ring circus,—and they needed a sort of a
cheap clown, so I joined them.

I heard from some of the neighbors that it looked bad,
owing to father's standing in the State as a man, but I went
ahead. I learned to sing the clown's song while standing on

a barrel, with brass band accompaniment, and at that I did
fairly well, if the band played loud; but Joe McMahan, the
manager of the circus, thought I ought to do more, so I
tried the spring-board. They had led up an old elephant and
a horse with spots on him. All the acrobats and tumblers ran

down this steep incline and hit the spring-board, and went up and turned from one to three somersaults, going over the elephant and horse, and lit on a big straw tick on the other side. My clown makeup consisted of a heavy, ponderous stomach, also made of straw. I'd never jumped on a spring-board, and no one explained to me the angles at which it was best to hit. I took a long run as I hit the spring-board. I evidently hit it too high up, and instead of going up over the elephant and horse, I cushioned back up the spring-board, lit on the back of my neck, and fell off among the brass band. It made a tremendous hit with the audience, notwithstanding that it nearly broke my neck. They applauded and applauded until they saw me being helped into the dressing room.

It made another clown jealous, as he didn't do anything half as funny that evening. It was some days before I recovered; but in a circus they use you all the time. While I was laid up with this stiff neck, I had to take care of the children that belonged to a husband and wife who were trapeze performers, and every time their act was called somebody had to mind the baby.

But somehow a fellow soon tires of circus life, and I came home and found that my drawing had improved some, as I had made lots of pictures in the circus. So, finally, father thought I had better go to San Francisco, as he said that was the art center for all the United States. So, the following winter, after it had been raining about a week, we commenced to get ready for the San Francisco trip.

People had been coming to the house all morning to say good-bye, and finally father came up from downtown carrying a valise. It was really a beautiful valise. He explained to me that it was better than these stiff dress-suit cases, as in case it became necessary, I could use it as a pillow. On one side of it was a scene in a garden, and on the

other side it showed the coast range mountains with a sunset. The handles were leather, but the rest of it was made of fine, thick cloth that looked like carpet.

It was nearly time for us to start when father thought perhaps the twenty-dollar gold piece I was taking with me had better not be carried in my pants pocket. So, owing to certain differences between San Francisco and Silverton, they thought it best to have me step behind the door and take off my coat and vest and shirt while they put the gold piece in a patch on my underclothes. They sewed it so that it practically lay on my right shoulder-blade, so that by moving my right arm I could tell whether my bank account was all right or not.

Father was always careful at figures and accurate in calculations, so he figured in giving me the change I was to have in my pockets, a day's allowance extra, in case of a washout, or something, and finally we started for the train. All along the streets were lined with people. Silverton, as I was likely seeing it for the last time, looked more beautiful than ever. The rain had dwindled down to a fine mist that didn't amount to anything. The people of the town were all smiles. I guess they looked better to me than I did to them. It was a bashful trip for me,

as I had left a few months before to be the artist on the *Oregonian* at Portland, and the whole town went into a half-holiday, and the streets were decorated. I even bid them good-bye for ever; but I was fired, and came back before some of the flower decorations had wilted. Thus it got to be a joke, and naturally the people thought we were foolish to let father spend so much money on such an uncertain trail, and I couldn't blame them.

But father,—God bless him,—he didn't comment one way or the other. He just carried the carpet-bag and kept a sad expression on his face. But Silverton came out to a man. The blacksmiths with their aprons on as they lined up in front of the shop looked like sculptors. The clerks in the stores looked as good as the proprietors themselves, and Ai Coolidge and Jake McClaine looked like the coast range mountains. Some of them made father's chin quiver a little when in their good advice they yelled, as they shook hands:

"Well, Homer, be a good boy and stick to it; don't ever come back!"

When we got through the heart of the town into the residence portion between houses, father looked me straight in the eyes and said:

"They meant well, but it sounded a little hard for us, didn't it?"

And no answer was necessary.

At each gate we said good-bye to the women of the family; and some of the girls I had seen traces of beauty in, now looked like goddesses and queens. But their advice was all about the same. The general tone was to stay away. Finally, near the depot, one old woman varied the advice by saying to me, as she shook hands:

"Homer, if you fail this time, come home and give up this here making pictures, and help your father work, as he's getting pretty old!"

Father went with me to Woodburn, ten miles below Silverton, where we were to catch the main line of the Southern Pacific. There we spent the whole afternoon waiting for the California overland that came about six in the evening.

We spent the time talking of what I should do when I got to San Francisco; of the great sights I must naturally see, as it was evidently to be different from Portland.

Finally we had only an hour more to wait for the train, and I got to thinking of this—that father had protected me from hard labor all of my life, simply because it had been my mother's wish that I should some day be a cartoonist. That this same man who had tried to educate me and who had wholly failed in his attempt, still took it good-naturedly; I thought of his kindness that, during sunshine and rain, sickness and good health, had always been just the same, willing and obliging, working hour after hour that he might enlighten me so that I could avoid some things that he had learned through hard knocks. I saw in him the finest type of the Western pioneer who had educated himself by his own efforts, who had come to Oregon in the early days; who had grown up with the State; who had been identified with its very earliest politics; who had risen in the esteem of his fellow-men to a high position; a man whose honor had never been questioned; a philosopher, a mathematician, a scientist, a poet,—in fact, the highest form of a scholar. He had been my champion against all comers who believed that I should have done manual labor, while he was satisfied if I would only draw pictures.

I was to leave this man perhaps forever, as his features commenced to show the letting down of the physical man that had made him so alert in the years past.

Finally we looked down the track toward Portland, and we could see the headlight on the engine that was to take me away. We had been holding hands for half an hour, and we hadn't spoken a word. Finally, turning to me, he said:

"Homer, I feel like the old farmer, and I guess you do, who was on his death-bed, when they sent for the minister. The old farmer hadn't been a church member in his day, hadn't given much thought to religion or the hereafter. When the preacher asked him as the family stood close around, if he wouldn't like to make his peace with God, he said, 'No, I don't see as there is any use, we ain't never had any fuss.'"

So, as the grip of our hands grew stronger, he said, "Homer, we've never had any fuss, so we can part peacefully."

On the train my valise attracted attention, and a crowd of drummers gathered around it. They asked me where I was going, and I told them to San Francisco. They asked me where I got the valise and I told them, and I saw a few of them take down the storekeeper's name that sold it. Finally one of them said, after I had told them my name: "Mr. Davenport, I don't think you appreciate the opening there is for you or anybody else in San Francisco with that kind of a valise." A few in the car laughed, but at that time I didn't see the joke. Finally one of the drummers said if I'd open and they got a look inside of it, he could tell if it was a real one. He said if the colors came clear through the cloth, it's real; if they don't, it's just an imitation. So I opened it and he put his head inside of it. He said: "Yes, it is a real one; they come all the way through."

I had never slept on a train, so, after I watched them take down a few berths, I went to bed just for the novelty of it, taking upper eight. In the middle of the night, a drummer who had got on the train after I had gone to bed, and was going to get off before I would be up in the morning, said that he would like to see that valise, if it was not too much trouble. So I dug it from under my pillow and showed it to him with the greatest of pride. I remember the drummer said he was sorry he wasn't going to San Francisco with me, but he said he wouldn't be there until the next week. I told him I guessed I'd remember him and should like to see him.

The next day across the mountains there were more drummers. Peanut butchers were now selling oranges that had taken the place of apples, and already you could notice quite a California air. With the assurance of how well they thought I'd do there and the sunshine that had taken the place of rain in Oregon, I was being a better fellow than I should, spending money more freely than I really needed to.

There was a gaiety in the smoking-car that I wasn't used to. The through passengers were all thoroughly acquainted with one another, and the second night I couldn't really sleep in upper eight. So I was thinking how great San Francisco would look, of what artists I would see there, and whether the general body of people on the streets would look so different from what they did in Portland. I got up before daylight, and, as the gray dawn came, I could see great streaks of yellow flowers out in the fields we were running through. The atmosphere was different, and I actually felt like an artist, if I could only draw.

Finally the train ran on to a ponderous ferry boat and was ferried across a river or bay and the closer we got to San Francisco, the faster the train ran; and as the conductor came through and gave each of us a ferry ticket to cross the bay from Oakland to San Francisco, I saw that I had spent the last cent of change father gave me,—that I had made it just a dead heat.

Aside from the twenty-dollar gold piece in my undershirt, I was completely out.

I wanted to get to the Murphy Building, in which building we had some friends living. A drummer put me on a car as it stood on the turn-table at the foot of Market Street. As this car rolled off the turn-table, I saw what a peculiar position I was in financially. When the conductor came for the fare, I told him that I had come from Oregon, that my father thought he gave me enough change to last until I got to San Francisco, but that he hadn't. That on my back, sewed in my underclothes, I had a twenty-dollar gold piece. That if he would let me off at the Murphy Building, I would get some change there, and pay him when his car came back. But he said gruffly: "I haven't the slightest doubt, after a look of your valise, that you have money sewed all over your clothes, but the company doesn't send us out with buttonhole shears, so you will have to get out your money."

I told him he could feel of it on my back, whereupon he did. Several passengers also volunteered; but I had to get off the car and, owing to the difference that San Francisco bore to Silverton, I lost several hours it seemed, hunting a suitable place that I might get to this twenty.

Finally, after I got the twenty, I went back and got on another car on the turn-table, and had ridden to about the same spot, when the conductor came through and I gave him my money. He informed me that they didn't make change for over five dollars. That I would have to get off and have it changed. It seemed that I never would get to the Murphy Building. I had gotten to San Francisco about eight o'clock in the morning, and now it was past noon, and I hadn't got away from the ferry. I lost more time trying to get change. Finally a man suggested that I buy a cigar. I foolishly told him I didn't smoke, and he suggested that I had better smoke, even to get my change.

Finally, with the change, I again proceeded to a car. This time I got on a blue car, told the conductor I wanted to get off at the Murphy Building. The car rolled up Market Street with the beautiful gliding, soothing noise. I don't think I have ever been so impressed or bewildered as I was by that ride. It seemed that I rode hours. Finally the car sheered off to the left and came to Eucalyptus Trees and then to Scant Settlement, and finally to the end of the line. Everybody got off but me, and the conductor said, "Oh, yes; you wanted to get off, didn't you?"

I said: "Yes, at the Murphy Building."

He said: "Stay on until we go back."

They came in, the conductor and gripman, and sat down and talked to me of where I had come from. They said they were bound to see a great deal of me, especially the gripman. I asked them how long they thought it would take a fellow to learn the city, and it seemed like the truth when they told me some people never learned it. Finally we started back toward town. Strange and beautiful faces got on the car, and finally I was lost again in admiration of the heart of the city, when everybody seemed to jump from the car and run for the ferryboat, and I noticed we were back to the turn-table. The conductor came through and said: "Oh, yes; you still want to get off at the Murphy Building." I said: "Yes, if I can get there before dark I'd like to; but if I can't, transfer me to a sleeper." He said: "All right now, set your valise up in your lap so that when I see it I will know you get off at the Murphy Building."

I saw him look in my direction once or twice, and I held the valise up at him; but he shook his head. Finally, just about dusk of what had been the most strenuous day of all my life, he put me off in front of the Murphy Building, and I lost no time in hurrying in.

Once in the Murphy Building the elevator man asked me first where I wanted to go, and I told him to see some people named Mr. and Mrs. Cline who lived somewhere on the top floor. So he took me up in the elevator, kind of showing off, I guess, by the way he ran it, as it didn't seem over a second till we were at the top, the sixth floor; and for fear some accident might happen and I would get astray, he led me to the Cline's very door.

Once inside, a few seconds after I had rapped, it was all over. We were home, and in their presence I felt safe. We visited for two or three hours as hard as people ever visit. Night had come but it didn't get dark. The glare from the street below seemed to light us up for miles. Finally, with their permission, I went to the front window and, with my forehead plastered against the pane, until it had stuck, I stood a good while looking down on Market Street below. It didn't seem possible that I would ever be able to walk down there alone; and, as I watched the traffic coming and going and saw the first signs of the real outside world, I thought and longed for Silverton, which seemed so far away.

THE END

WHEN DAVENPORT'S IN SILVERTON.
(BY JAMES J. MONTAGUE.)

They're all awake in Silverton, although it's half past eight,
And gapes and yawns betray the fact that is mighty late;
The lamp is lit in Wolfard's store, and Simeral and all
The rest are tilted back in chairs, around the stove and wall.
Saliva hisses on the hearth, and through the open door
Come citizens and cats and dogs until they fill the store;
And on the street the whisper runs like magic up and down:
"Le's all go up to Wolfard's store, f'r Davenport's in town."

Without a word the old-time friends from almost everywhere
Come dropping in and occupy each cracker box and chair;
And though the clock ticks on and on, until it's nearly ten,
They never stir, but hungrily live o'er the past again.
The time the dog—of worthless life—was chucked inside a sack
And dropped by night in Silver Creek, and came serenely back
The time the famous Trombone Band won Silverton renown,
Are all discussed, and all enjoyed, when Davenport's in town.

They do not care in Silverton much for the world outside,
They little know this loved friend is honored far and wide,
They do not know, nor do they care, what Eastern people say,
They only know that Davenport has come to town to-day.
And sitting breathless 'round that stove they listen to him tell
About the days before he bade old Silverton farewell.
To them it matters not at all, if fate may smile or frown
It's quite enough for Silverton that Davenport's in town.

BOOKS BY
HOMER DAVENPORT

Cartoons
1898

The Dollar or the Man
1900

My Quest of the Arabian Horse
published by B.W. Dodge & Company
New York, 1909

The Country Boy
originally published by G.W. Dillingham Company
New York, 1910

BOOKS ON
HOMER DAVENPORT

Homer Davenport of Silverton
by Leland Huot and Alfred Powers

Homer: The Country Boy
by Mickey Hickman

Powell's Press

Located in Portland, Oregon, Powell's Press is committed to finding titles currently out of print by renowned Oregon authors and making them once again available nationally. Powell's Press is a division of Powell's Books Inc., whose flagship store, Powell's City of Books, is the world's largest used and new bookstore. You can order Powell's Press books (and over a million other titles) by visiting *powells.com*.

The Oregon Cultural Heritage Commission discovers, celebrates and commemorates contributions to Oregon's diverse literary and cultural legacy, raising awareness through publications and other media, memorials, and public events. OCHC programs, including three nationally attended symposiums, have featured presentations on cultural figures including Hazel Hall, C.E.S. Wood, John Reed, Louise Bryant, Abigail Scott Duniway, James Beard, Opal Whiteley, Stewart Holbrook, H.L. Davis, and dozens more. Our interests focus on figures from all the arts that make up the creative cultural history of the Pacific Northwest. For more information, please reach us at: OCHC, PO Box 3588, Portland, OR 97208 or encanto@teleport.com.

Printed in the United States
913800001B